GERALDINE MOORKENS BYRNE

The Body Politic

Caroline Jordan Series Book 1

For Mark, because everything.
And for Dara and Fiachra who are also, everything.

Contents

Foreword

The Body Politic is set in 2010, as the recession tightens its grip on Ireland and the boom era of the Celtic Tiger draws to an end. I have invented politicians like Michael T O'Mahony and Derek Fields; they are the leadership we needed but didn't actually receive. They are wholly fictional characters.

The places mentioned like Leinster House, the Dáil (the Irish Parliament) and various other offices and venues are either real or represent real places. I like to think if you ever make it to Dublin, you'll recognize some of its most iconic areas after reading the Caroline Jordan Series.

I've added a glossary to help with some of the Irish terms and slang, although to date no one has had much trouble with it. As this is a traditional-style Murder Mystery, the language is modern but not overly offensive. Bear in mind Irish and UK spellings are used throughout. I hope you have fun reading about Caroline Jordan and her world.

Acknowledgement

I've been playing around with Caroline Jordan for a few years now, and over that time have had critical input, emotional support and a lot of tolerant forbearance from friends and family. Especially deserving of praise are my family, especially my husband. No man deserves to be woken in the middle of the night by questions such as "How would you get enough nicotine to kill someone?"

And to my mother Maria Moorkens Byrne, who is an inspiration. I have lovely cousins, all of them, who keep telling me they like what I write. I am blessed in my in-laws, who are generally my biggest cheerleaders.

I have friends who have supported me and whose patience in reading, commenting, critiquing and encouraging have made all the difference in completing every poem, every article and now this book. I appreciate every one of you and have to thank Gina and Emer especially for just generally being my wings, when I can't fly myself. My circle of Wagons too - thanks Marie, Edda and Kristen.

And to the rest, too many to mention, thanks and gratitude.

GLOSSARY

Irish Terms and Slang

An Taoiseach - The Irish word for Prime Minister, pronounced " On Tee-Shock" meaning Leader.

Dail- the Irish parliament, pronounced Dawl

Leinster House - the common name for the Houses of Parliament in Ireland, where the Seanad (senate) and Dail (parliament) Sit

Seanad - Pronounced Shan-id this is the second House of the Irish Parliament, and with the President (titular head of Ireland) and the Dail it forms the government. It has limited legislative power but is intended to be an extra oversight, and can introduce legislation as well as delay it (not veto it.)

The President of Ireland is a titular head. The Taoiseach is the actual political leader. Presidents have 8 year terms. In recent years we have had two female presidents, hugely well regarded internationally and now have the Poet Statesman Michael D Higgins, who remains our most popular president to date.

De Valera, one of the early founders of the Irish State, who set an image for the country of pure catholic Ireland, maidens dancing at crossroads etc (Spoiler, he wasn't that nice.)

SLANG

Amadán - an eejit

Eejit- a right Gobdaw

Gobdaw - a total Amadán

All three mean a gormless, foolish person

also **Git, Git face**

Skanger - a rough, (usually) young person, up to no good
  Auld - old
  Auld wan - old person (f)
  Auld Fella - old person (m)
  hissy fit - temper tantrum
  holliers - holidays
  craic - fun
  janey mac- typical Dublin expression of surprise
  a dote - a lovely person
  Dote on - very fond of
  Culchie - pro "Cull-cheee" Anyone not from Dublin
  Jackeen - anyone from Dublin

THE BODY POLITIC

Geraldine Moorkens Byrne

1

Chapter One

Caroline Jordan – a very bad day

"I'm afraid we have some bad news for you, Ms. Jordan. Minister Fitzpatrick passed away some time last night."

The room was silent for a long moment while the police officer – Garda, we say in Ireland – looked at me expectantly. I had no idea what to say, and I'm an expert in saying the most appropriate thing at the right moment. I even get paid for it.

But for once, my Public Relations inspiration didn't strike. We all stood staring at each other until eventually my colleague broke the silence.

"Into every life, a little rain must fall..." Mark Jacobs murmured sadly, careful not to meet my eye.

I couldn't help but feel it was a slightly inappropriate response to the news that our beloved leader, politician and statesman Damian Fitzpatrick had passed away. It was also insincere. Neither of us could pretend to be especially upset at his demise, personally.

I heard a rumour later that the man's own brother had said it wasn't much of a loss. Liam was a dote of a man, unlike his brother, so it's unlikely he actually said it, but I bet he thought it very, very loudly.

The news would soon be filled with reports on his demise, I thought. Constituency offices and ministries would be flooded with tearful tributes from the party faithful. Even his political adversaries would be shedding tears at his passing and a lot of "We will never see his like again," type comments would be dusted off.

In fact, probably the only people left unmoved would be those of us who actually knew him. Let's just say, Fitzpatrick had undoubtedly been a very difficult man in private.

I tried not to look at his desk, where the body had been found, slumped across it. Damian had occupied one of the ministerial offices in the heart of Leinster House, the once ducal palace that had housed the Irish parliament since 1922.

While the actual department – Justice – operated out of buildings a short walk away on St Stephen's Green, Damian had spent most of his time closer to the seat of power in the Dáil itself. His great ambition had been to make that walk across the corridor to Government Buildings, to the Oak paneled office that sheltered the leader of the country, An Taoiseach.

In the meantime, he'd furnished his office with the taste and budget of a tinpot dictator. I knew for a fact that his desk cost my yearly salary, while the artwork was twice as costly.

Take, for example, one large oil painting by the famously lecherous artist, Philip McMahon, entitled "Maiden yielding to temptation" It depicted a rotund, fresh faced, neoclassical young wan on the verge of falling into the arms of an older man.

It cost over €30,000 and I am being kind when I say you wouldn't hang it in your loo.

Damian's heart attack was certainly a shock...

("suddenly, without warning, mourned by all, tragic loss to the country," – my years in Public Relations and Media had given me the bad habit of mentally writing press releases on every event.)

But considering his tendency to work himself up into apoplectic rages at the drop of a hat, no one could be terribly surprised.

What did surprise me was that he died of natural causes; I would have laid good money on him being murdered someday. Charming, and professorial in public or in front of a TV camera, he was pure evil in private – the previous four years of employment as his press secretary had been the worst years of employment I had ever experienced.

Only the fact that Damian had also made them the most lucrative years I had ever worked, had stopped me from staving his head in with a paperweight myself on occasion.

"Miss Jordan?" I realized that everyone in the room, from my colleague, Mark Jacobs, to the two plain-clothes Gardaí, was staring at me. I summoned a look of distress and my best fluttering female voice.

"I'm so sorry. It's all just such a dreadful shock…. you were saying?"

Mark shot me a look of pure disgust; he knew I had hated Damian as much as he did, and that I was about as distressed as a lottery winner. He also knew I was as far from a fluttering female as a Black Widow Spider.

But I was the Public Relations Consultant, and I was expected to lie, whereas as a pensioned, pampered civil servant he could afford to be more honest. The older of the two Gardaí gave me a sympathetic look but the younger one – Detective Sergeant Doyle, if I recalled correctly – didn't seem too convinced.

"I asked, when did you last see the Minister?" He wasn't exactly truculent, but he was brusque.

This was a little tricky. I was not morally opposed to lying in general, but I had made it a rule up until now, to not actually lie to the police.

The problem with moments like this is that you really have such a short amount of time to decide which road to take. Tell the truth, tell a lie. Look stupid or risk looking guilty further down the line. I like to think I would have told the truth if it had not involved a third party. I think I would have said "About half nine, he was sitting at his desk" but instead I gave an alternative version of events.

That is after all my job – to present alternative versions of what someone meant, what the minister intended, how something should have sounded… so I said "I saw him at 6.45. I left early you see. He was still here when I left."

Every word strictly true of course. Not quite a lie, then. I feel so much better.

How was Damian's wife taking it, I wondered idly while the Garda took note of my answer. I imagined she was playing an excellent Widow of the Nation but privately, she had to be dancing a jig. It was an open secret in political circles that Damian Fitzpatrick had at least two long-term mistresses; though like most Irish politicians, he played the catholic family man.

Post Celtic Tiger Ireland may like Sex and Scandal, but we want our politicians as pure as De Valera. Especially in these days of austerity – no one wants to think that their ministers are drinking champagne and running riot with floozies on the country's money, while the rest of us makeshift with leftovers and a few pints once a month.

The older Garda glanced at his notes, reading them through carefully. His appearance and demeanour screamed Special Branch; working in the parliament buildings, you got to know the look of them very quickly. "Mr. Jacobs, you left the Minister at 8.45, am I right?"

"Yes," Mark had obviously gone over this before, judging by his thinly veiled impatience, "It was 8.45 give or take five minutes. I didn't take a particular note of the time, you understand. But it was in or around a quarter to or ten to the hour."

The Special Branch man nodded and returned to his notes. The other one fixed Mark with a steely look and remarked "It seems late for a civil servant to be working…. a quarter to nine at night."

Both Mark and I snorted. "Late?"

"Contrary to public perception, Garda, politicians work early and late, and their staff work with them. Especially incumbent Ministers in a possibly outgoing administration; there are any number of loose ends to tie up. We've been working all hours these last few months."

Mark managed to sound like the picture of outraged virtue, the civil servant whose very health and well-being were sacrificed regularly on the altar of the nation's good.

He might be overdoing it a trifle but not by much.

Considering the current state of the country – recession, bank crises, and expense scandals – any politician who wanted a shout at his seat in the next general election had his PR and press team working overtime. The cynical might suggest that it would be more productive for him to actually work overtime, but that's just not how it works around here.

You could single-highhandedly solve the banking crisis, save the whale and reverse global warming but without the likes of me and my team, you wouldn't get a paragraph in the Evening Herald.

Mark, being our beloved leader's private secretary, got to stay late and brainstorm with us on occasion; especially before big announcements or even more importantly, when we try to avoid unwanted announcements.

So far in my 4 years as Fitzpatrick's PR and media whore, I'd averted at least 6 major scandals, spun several of his irrational rages as "passionate concern for the issues" and done my best to keep his goody-two-shoes image alive and well. I was reasonably sure I was not popular as a result.

Mark had been around much longer than I and he practically ran the place. He used to be in Environment, he had touched on every department at one stage or another in his career, and he tended to make friends rather than enemies among his colleagues, so really, he had a hand in everything.

"Has anyone told the Taoiseach?" Mark asked suddenly. The Gardaí exchanged a look.

Declan had been both the Grand Old Man of the party and a bitter rival to the Taoiseach, the Irish prime minister, although both hotly denied any antagonism. We had frequently endured the deceased Minister for Justice's vicious ranting against our urbane, charming Taoiseach – the press loved him even more than goody-goody Fitzpatrick which drove the Minister insane with jealousy.

I imagined Michael T O'Mahony dancing around his office and embracing the Gardaí who broke the news to him.

"Yes," the older of the detectives said carefully. "I believe he is fully apprised of the situation."

That was probably Special Branch for "He's popped the champagne and is dancing on the desk."

His colleague snapped his notebook shut and growled "Well that's all I suppose." He turned rather cold blue eyes on me and asked pointedly "You're quite sure about the time then, Miss?"

"I am" I said firmly. The cheek of him, sounding like he didn't believe me. I mean, obviously, I wasn't quite being honest, but he didn't know that.

2

Chapter Two

The two Gardaí took their leave and I sat down on the nearest chair fighting the urge to cry. Shock, not grief. So, there we were.

"PR guru out on her ear" the little headline editor in my head hissed. I had to admit that far from mourning the old git I was far more concerned with my own plight. Here I was, 35 or thereabouts, unexpectedly ousted from a high-profile job.

In an ideal world, or if this were a romantic story, I would welcome the release from the shallow and cynical world of politics. Retreating to the wilds of rural Ireland I would discover nature and a talent for painting or making soap or some twittery like that. Anyway, I would shun those parties and press releases and journalists sucking up to me for a story. But obviously, I wouldn't have gone into PR in the first place if I had any objection to shallow and cynical.

The job had its drawbacks (Damian Fitzpatrick for example), but it had its compensations; I was on the guest list of a hundred venues, I was invited to every social event from balls to dinner parties and while I was not exactly facing a lifetime in the wilderness, there was no denying that my stock would fall sharply once I left Leinster House.

I remembered the first day I had strolled through those hallowed gates and had my bags searched by security. The bitchy comments, the sexist remarks from the Old Boy's Club. The pleasure of sticking the knife into the same misogynistic troglodytes later on, when they had to come crawling for my advice or influence with Fitzpatrick. Ah, happy memories.

The old part of the House might be crumbling, the sprawling complex of offices might be a confusing mess, but no one could deny the hold this place had over those working here. It was a heady mix of history and current affairs and idealism and cynicism. Every time I was summoned, I felt a bit more important. That my tiny firm had won this contract, right out from under the snooty noses of established PR gurus, was my proudest achievement.

Plus, there was the small question of finances. At the height of the Celtic Tiger boom, I'd been working in Dublin's largest PR firm, and the idea to go out on my own had seemed brave, entrepreneurial, and forward thinking.

Now it seemed suicidal.

I had bank loans, wage bills and the rest of my disposable income went on my mortgage (a shoe-box apartment in Dublin's trendiest apartment block.) Oh, and my wardrobe. I spent an awful lot on clothes which frankly I resented because I don't even like fashion that much, but I was stuck.

No, I really was. Don't be so judgmental.

You cannot wear a unique outfit twice in a given time frame, you really can't. Not when it's your job to look a certain way. And I wasn't extravagant – my wardrobe was full of classic items that could be mixed and matched and tread a fine line between designer labels and bargains. And I only owned a normal sane person's number of shoes. I loathed and detested women who treated footwear like religion.

"You spent far too much on takeaways and eating out," my long-suffering accountant Jennie pointed out last April.

"But on the other hand, I haven't had a holiday in over three years!" It was true, barely a freaking weekend off never mind a trip.

But whatever the excuses, the fact remained I couldn't afford to lose my lead client and the kudos that went with it. My other contracts, handled by my juniors Paula and Stephen, wouldn't keep all three of us in Vodka. It was a horrible feeling, realizing that if the stupid old fool had managed to not have a heart attack, I wouldn't be facing financial ruin. Even from beyond the grave Damian Fitzpatrick was screwing with me.

I sat at my desk in my lovely Kildare Street office and listened to the muted gossiping along the corridors of power. Stop panicking, Start thinking – my mantra for dealing with any threatened crisis came to mind.

Whatever else, my name was known, and my work was respected by those in the know. For the next three or four weeks, people would want the cachet of knowing someone on the inside, so they could garner details of the demise and burial of my erstwhile boss. I could surely leverage that into at least a couple of meetings and more contracts. Once the funeral was over -

The funeral! What on earth was I thinking? I reached for my mobile with one hand while frantically searching through my folders with the other.

Damian Fitzpatrick's wife Margaret (Margo to her lackeys, but only behind her back when they were sure she wasn't within a two-mile radius) was not the type to have organized the funeral herself.

With any luck, she was too busy dabbing at her eyes and practicing her "Poor Widda Woman" look to have thought of the funeral. If I could get in there first, and assume command, it would be the perfect opportunity for one last showcase of my talents. A discreet way of saying "Gun for hire, I can make even Damian Fitzpatrick look saintly."

Admittedly he had to be dead to make sure of it, but I had not done too bad a job while he was alive either.

Margo answered on the third ring. I was half surprised that she answered herself; I thought she would have delegated call screening to one of her many daughters-in-law. Margaret Fitzpatrick had five sons, all cheerful rugby playing types and all bar one was married and had provided her with a brood of cheerful, middle-class, rugby playing grandchildren.

Of course, Margaret suffered from chronic insecurity at the best of times, always anxious that no other political wife or socialite stole a march on her. She probably feared one of her offspring or their spouse giving an impromptu interview over the phone to one of the tabloids.

Just be glad you've caught her, I reminded myself. I pitched my voice somewhere between distraught employee and concerned friend.

"Oh Margaret... Trailing off as if I just didn't know what to say would get her, I knew. She viewed me as slick and glib, and she would be on the lookout for any hint that I saw through her grieving façade to the cynical wagon beneath.

Possibly she would guess that I was about as affected as her youngest grandson's pet tortoise, but it didn't matter, as long as we both agreed to make believe.

"Oh Caroline…" Margaret had worked hard to cover her country roots. She was what we Dubliners termed a "culchie" -anyone not lucky enough to be born in Dublin, really. But no one would now recognize a hint of her native Leitrim in her carefully neutral accent. "How are you, how are you?"

Brave widow concerned with the feelings of others, despite her own grief, my treacherous brain whispered.

"I'm – carefully timed pause- doing okay. But never mind me, for goodness sake. How are you? I just can't imagine what you're going through! I'm so very, very sorry."

(Thus, establishing her as Queen of the Drama, and paying tribute to her privileged status.)

"Oh Caroline…I can't tell you; I can't begin to explain!" But she proceeded to do just that for five tedious minutes, while I made soothing noises and drew on my telephone pad. When she had fully exhausted her flow of clichéd grief, the opportunity arose to strike.

"Well, I know there's very little I can do or say that will make this any better for you, but I just wanted you to know I'm here and I'm on your side."

There was a delicious moment of silence as that sank in; then, hesitantly "On my side?"

"Oh yes, don't you worry. I have your back. You know what those creeping snakes are like – I've had four journo scum on already asking about the funeral, is it just going to be local, is it true O'Mahony won't attend, Is the president coming home from abroad, that kind of crap."

"Oh my god" she said faintly.

"Oh, don't you worry," I replied. "I told them nothing, except that it's all in hand. O'Mahony won't dare not attend, I'll sort him out. I've already been onto the office and the president is flying home from her holiday."

Yes, yes, I know – I am a bad woman and will die roaring.

"Oh, thank you Caroline! You're such a rock!" Her relief was genuine – any hint that the funeral would be less than stately, would have spell disaster socially for her. And for any of her fresh-faced offspring who planned on stepping into Daddy's shoes.

"Not at all, Margaret. It's the least I can do, the very least. I'll have all the options for you by this evening, so you can look at it whenever you feel able. All I'll need from you is the personal touch – after all, no one could possibly know Damian the way you do. And the boys, of course."

"You're so right, "she said a shade too eagerly. The insecurity was setting in already. "No one knew him like I did. No one. Caroline dear, could you call over tomorrow morning and we'll go through everything? Oh wonderful, wonderful. I know the children will be delighted to know they can leave everything in your hands. Such a rock. And if any more of those nasty journalists ring…"

"I'll tell them I have everything in hand and details will be announced in due time."

"In due time. Yes, I like that."

It took a few more minutes of soothing and hand-holding before I could safely hang up. I barely had her cut off before I speed dialed the offices of Jordan PR and cut through Paula's "receptionist" spiel. We were small firm, you understand and couldn't afford an actual receptionist, so Paula and Stephen took turns at pretending.

"Paula, I need a press release, asap. Every paper, national, red tops, RTE, TV3 – everything. Get onto that orange-faced desk monkey in Radio One, as well. Jordan PR is handling all the details of Damian Fitzpatrick's funeral. That's the main message, just dress it up in the usual "the family of the deceased request that you honour their privacy at this painful moment" sort of crap."

I love Paula, she never wasted time asking questions or complicating matters. Even as I spoke, I could hear her clicking away at her desktop; that press release was as good as written.

"Remember, we're close personal friends, I'm a colleague, this is a labour of love and at the family's request." I warned her.

I knew she'd find some way to work it in. I also knew I didn't have to spell out to her how important this was for her, for all of us, for Jordan PR.

3

Chapter Three

DS Alan Doyle.

One of the many complaints my ex-girlfriend leveled at me was that I had no people skills, other than interrogating them.

I never really thought much about it – Karen had a litany of complaints against me by the end, they all blurred together – but then my first duty sergeant took me aside and warned me about it.

That's when it dawned on me then that it might be true. It isn't deliberate – I just don't really get small talk and to be honest if someone can't answer a straight question it makes me wonder about them.

But you can't get ahead if everyone you come into contact with complains about your manner, so I learned to curb what Karen called my "more aggressive traits," or I called, my personality.

I always knew I would end up in either Serious Crimes or Special Branch and that was my goal from the day I joined. Special branch was sort of a natural home for me – my dad had been a member for the last 15 years of his career. When I made detective – the second youngest Garda in the history of the state to do so – he was delighted.

My mother was pleased if slightly resigned; I think she rather felt that having put in 30 years worrying about my father on the job, it would have been nice if I had become a geography teacher or something. It was a feeling shared by every woman I have ever dated as well.

The one really serious relationship of my late twenties– that would be Karen again – started because she liked me in my uniform and ended because she spent the next six years resenting the job.

Anyway, as luck would have it, when I joined Special Branch, they were in the process of forming a specialist squad.

It was designed to deal with the kind of sensitive, scandal laden messes that seemed to plague modern Irish politics. Sometimes it was dealing with a historical crime – what the yanks call cold cases – covered up for decades by high-ranking politicians. Sometimes it was finding out where the vectors of crime and politics crossed – where the plain brown envelopes filled with cash, or the trail of favours and contracts and land deals led.

And sometimes it was murder.

Technically code-named the Specialist Crimes "S" unit, we are generally known as the Specially Career-ending Suspects Unit. Yeah, we're hilarious. That's grade A cop humour, right there.

But as a Special Branch detective, I was pretty much allowed be myself. If a delicate charming hand was needed, they sent someone like David Locke, who could wheedle his way in anywhere and once became best friends with a terrorist suspect's own mother. The suspect arrived home unexpectedly to find David being served Sunday dinner.

On the other hand, if they needed a suspicious brain and closed mouth, or a brusque tongue, which would be my forte.

When DS Graves (aka Tombstone, partly because of the name and partly because he has front teeth like slabs) called me in and told me we were off to investigate the untimely demise of the Minister for Justice, I expected a straightforward case.

The man had a heart attack and keeled over, sadly there was no one around to help as it was late enough – 8.30 pm at the earliest and more than likely between 9 pm and 9.30 pm. The cleaners arrived at 9.50. The last of the civil service staff left at 8.45 and he was fairly sure the Minister was moving around his office at that time.

See, simple.

Except from the moment we arrived, it all went wrong. Graves is a good man and a respected unit leader and thank heavens it was him, not one of the less experienced fellas in the squad because we had to think on our feet and show nothing.

When we arrived, the Minister was slumped across his desk, one hand hanging by his side and the other clamped to his chest, trapped under the body. The room was in darkness, the blinds having been drawn against the early October evenings and the only lights on were the green lamp on his mahogany desk and the muted glow of an elegant gold-stemmed standing lamp in one corner.

There were a selection of armchairs (leather) and several straight-backed hard chairs, on one of which was seated a weeping polish woman called Viktoria. She was the cleaner who had discovered the body.

She was accompanied by her supervisor, another Pole called Illa who spoke perfect English with a slight accent and a security guard called Nick Fallon, whom I had met before. He was a man in late middle age who practically ran the place single-handedly; if you needed something, you went to Nick.

Shortly after our arrival, the Private Secretary Mark Jacobs appeared, looking shocked and slightly disheveled. He was properly dressed in his suit and tie, the daily civil service uniform – dark grey pinstripe suit, white shirt, complementary tie – but he looked as if he'd thrown it back on in a hurry.

Graves was taken aside by Dr Lorraine O'Toole almost the moment she began to examine the body. A Minister of state dead at his desk called for the top forensic pathologist; even though the doctor whom the security staff had called seemed happy enough to sign off on heart attack.

I could see his face change as she spoke, rapidly and urgently. He glanced over his shoulder at the unfortunate Minister and then at me, and that look spoke volumes. I sighed and extricated myself from the voluble and agitated Viktoria; by the time I crossed the room to where the pathologist and Graves were huddled, Dr Lorraine was reaching for her mobile phone. Graves stopped her sharply.

"Doyle, there's a problem," he said tersely. "Get them out of here and clear the corridor. Act as if it's normal procedure. And ring the office, tell them we need the works."

Dr O'Toole was adamant. "I can't give an absolute opinion until I get him into the Lab, but this is not a heart attack." She pointed at the back of the neck, to a small, bruised area. "That, for a start. I'm sorry, gentlemen but this is a crime scene."

They were discreet but relentless, Lorraine's team were renowned for putting the forensics above everything else. Within an hour, the place was crawling with silent, hazard-suited techs, all working under the State pathologist's quiet but unquestionable authority.

Graves busied himself talking to the witnesses, and I saw him taking copious notes from Nick Fallon. As far as I could tell, no one seemed worried or disturbed by the presence of Forensics. To her credit, Lorraine looked as if it was an everyday occurrence to examine a Ministerial office.

The door opened and my boss, Finbar Looney, slipped in. I knew we were in the big shit now, because the last time Looney left the office to attend a crime scene, De Valera was in power.

He stood and stared around him with distaste. If there was one thing Looney hated, it was an unsolved crime, and one that involved politicians or public figures was a red rag to him. It didn't matter that we had only just discovered the crime; from now on in, we were on a ticking clock as far as he was concerned.

The irony was, everyone in the squad was handpicked and carefully vetted except our glorious leader. He was given S squad solely because of his ability to lick up to anyone above him in the chain of command. He could be relied upon to beat us serfs until the job was done.

Another huddled conference ensued and then Graves decided to drop the other shoe.

"I have a list of everyone in the building at the time. You won't like it."

"I take it you're not going to say a couple of cleaners and a security guard." Looney sighed.

"Well, yes but also just down the corridor we have An Taoiseach, Michael T O'Mahony, plus Derek Fields."

I could tell by the way Looney winced that the name Fields meant something to him. Graves continued, "Also, Minister Lillian Roche and her secretary Catherine Walsh. We also have three senior civil servants, but they were at least at the other side of the building."

"Then there were a couple of lobbyists in having a meeting with none other than the Minister for the Environment and his team of bicycle loving, desk jockeys." Graves despised cyclists, a legacy of his early days in Traffic. "Any one of them, in fact all of them, should be considered a suspect."

"Well not necessarily," Looney snapped. "With any luck, the Taoiseach and his meeting – who did you say? Lillian Roche and Derek Fields?"

"And Roche's secretary."

"Well with any luck they can be each other's alibis."

"Eh – it's not looking that way."

"What do you mean?"

"Well, I was talking to Nick Fallon earlier, just getting a feel for the comings and goings around here today and he told me Roche's meeting with the Taoiseach broke up briefly around 8.45." Graves consulted his notes.

"She stormed out and went ranting down the corridor, then no one could find her for half an hour. While Catherine Walsh was wandering around looking for her boss, the Taoiseach and his spin doctor were in the offices just down here."

Graves indicated on a crudely drawn map the rough distance from the Offices of An Taoiseach to those of the Minister in this building.

"Then shortly before nine, Fallon heard the Taoiseach and Fields talking on the stairwell. He couldn't hear what was said but he does know that one of them went downstairs and the other kept going along the corridor."

"Oh, for the love of …"

"It's as bad as it can get, assuming the good doctor hasn't made some horrible mistake. We have several high-ranking Ministers wandering around, along with senior civil servants, and An Taoiseach himself."

There was complete silence while Looney digested this. Graves and I stared at the floor and waited; Looney would come up with a plan of action but right now he was literally seething with rage that this stupidity could have happened at all, and if the murderer had appeared in front of us begging forgiveness and carrying his own signed confession, I wouldn't have given a halfpenny for his chances of surviving the Wrath of Finbar.

So, the best course of action for the innocent bystander right now was to remain quiet and let the boss's brain work it out for himself.

"Right," Looney suddenly clapped his hands and straightened up. "Heart Attack it is, at least for the moment. I need to take some advice on all this."

That meant going one step up, to Superintendent Mitch Fellows. "This is politics, boys, politics. God help us all."

He spun around on poor Dr Lorraine. "Silence, Doctor, that's the ticket. This is an absolute imperative. Silence."

The Pathologist shrugged. "I've gathered what we can in evidence, Finbar" she said, not a bit impressed by his bluster. "there'll have to be a Postmortem, of course."

Looney gave her a look that was half sardonic and half apologetic. "I wouldn't bet on it, Doctor. Not that I'm a betting man."

And so it went. No one questioned it, no one even asked that many questions. Damian Fitzpatrick was a womanizing, hard-drinking, cigar-smoking hedonist and a heart attack was probably the most likely end for him.

Added to this the almost universal undercurrent of dislike whenever the man's name was mentioned, and everyone seemed only too happy to let it be. His personal under-secretary, Jacobs, could barely conceal his contempt for the man.

I thought once or twice he seemed on the verge of saying something interesting, especially when we asked about the Minister's movements that evening, but it was only a hunch and as we were supposed to be conducting only routine inquiries on a natural death, I couldn't exactly press the man either.

We did what we could that night and got back at the crack of dawn the following morning. That's when Caroline Jordan first appeared; and what an impression she made. Like Jacobs, she had placed some veneer of decorum over her feelings, but it was obvious that she couldn't have cared less for the dead man. Before she had arrived, Catherine Walsh had mentioned her to Graves in somewhat scathing terms – tough, pushy and opinionated. And very ambitious.

One look at Jordan, a hard-faced piece, and I could imagine her using her famous and powerful boss as a stepping-stone. Half the time we interviewed her she looked as if she was busy writing a press release in her head. The other half she spent exchanging looks with Jacobs and making snide comments.

Graves didn't quite agree with me, despite what Walsh told him. "I thought she seemed quite nice," he grinned. "She liked me, anyway."

"Well, she goes for older fat baldy men," David Locke said, pointing to a picture of Fitzpatrick taken at some election count. "You're definitely in with a shout."

He snorted at our blank faces. "Ah come on boys, did you not guess? It's common knowledge Fitzpatrick has more than one bit on the side. How else do you think some PR girl no one ever heard of got this gig?"

Like I said, she didn't make a good impression.

The more we poured over the logistics of what happened that night before the Minister died, the worse it got. Lorraine came back with a verdict of murder – the deceased had been injected in the back of the neck with a solution of nicotine, the small bruise caused by a thumb being pressed down as the killer held his head in place. She had of course performed a Postmortem, despite Looney's desperate attempt to avoid it.

"I think he was sitting at the desk, maybe writing, maybe reading something closely. His head would have been bent slightly, the killer walks behind with the solution ready to inject, grasps firmly and inserts the needle."

"Boy or girl?" Graves asked.

"Either. Male is slightly more likely, in terms of holding the man in place and not allowing him to struggle but a woman who was familiar with him could have stroked the back of his neck and touched him – by the time he would have realized what was happening, it would have been too late."

"So," Locke said. "Essentially it could have been any of them."

"Nicotine…where would they get it?"

"Internet." Locke gestured wearily at his computer, which ironically enough, didn't have access to the internet. "You can google how to build a bomb these days, never mind how to extract nicotine and murder someone."

Graves, Locke, Darren Powers, Claire MacPherson and I had commandeered a small incident room. The doors were locked, and the blinds were down – it would have been laughable if it any less serious.

"This is a disaster." MacPherson almost growled in frustration. "You know we are supposed to have this done and dusted before Looney has a heart attack himself. But we have nothing. Not unless we start treating it like a normal murder scene and interview the people present."

She had a point; in any other circumstances by now we would have had the place clamped down, anyone who had been in the building would have been thoroughly investigated and the various alibis and lies and half-truths dismantled and examined one by one. Instead of which we were paralyzed.

"Looney's in with the lawyers now." Powers, one of our young go-getters, stretched and cracked every knuckle in his hand, to a chorus of groans.

"Yeah, can you imagine the question - Is it actually constitutional to investigate the Taoiseach for murder, while keeping the fact of the murder secret, while acknowledging the Taoiseach as a suspect who should not yet be told that we know it was murder?"

Graves shrugged. "Probably. Or not. Either way, I've a feeling it won't be Looney taking the blame."

"I'm glad I'm just a humble Garda," MacPherson grinned.

"Apparently, it is constitutional." Looney ran a hand over his face. He looked about ten years older than he had that morning.

"Seriously?"

"Yes." He said shortly. "What we have to decide now is whether to let slip that we know it was murder, and risk alerting a very dangerous and ruthless criminal. Or whether we should simply continue with the charade that Damian Fitzpatrick died of natural causes?" without waiting for an answer he added "Discretion, whatever else. Get out there and get answers, any damn way you can. But don't let me hear you've upset the Ministers or God forbid, the Taoiseach."

So solve it, without letting anyone know it happened. This was not shaping up to be my favourite investigation.

4

Chapter Four

Caroline Jordan

The week after Fitzpatrick's untimely demise was surreal. As much planning went into that funeral as into any society wedding or fashion launch and with far too many similarities not to feel that it was all a bit of a mad joke.

Of course, at this point I thought all was well – the thought of foul play wasn't even a twinkle in some pathologist's eye, as far as I knew, the poor deluded fool that I was.

All I was concerned with was putting on a grand, statesmanlike display and hopefully saving Jordan PR in the process.

The first thing was to jostle the hero, O'Mahony into a prime position in the service; he was as skittish as a colt about it all.

The problem from his point of view was that if he took too prominent a position, his political enemies would accuse him of trying to make hay out of his Minister's death. But from our point of view, we wanted him front and centre and looking as if he'd lost his only true friend.

In the end, it was Stephen who gently talked him into it, cleverly and calmly referring to him at all times as "such a special friend" to the family, "standing in such a unique relationship – not only colleague but party leader, not only leader but friend" until O'Mahony himself began to miss the old buzzard.

The President, bless her immaculate soul, was of course coming back for

21

the funeral; she was a lady to her fingertips and knew what was expected of her. All we had to do there was send a file around with the details and her staff followed up on it like civilized people, not the half-trained savages you got around the Dáil.

Once we had the leader, all the little sheep followed – there were TDs coming up for the funeral who rarely if ever showed up for voting. That took care of the politicos, which left the socialites.

If politics was male dominated, the social side of the funeral was still the stalking ground of the women, every one of them easily as power crazed as the men. It was a minefield; these were people who could hold grudge until judgment day. And you never knew who would end up on the board of some charity and be in a position to award you that lovely contract. So, it's a case of never saying "no" – but you can't say yes to everyone. This is the PR woman's conundrum.

It wasn't helped by the fact that the deceased left two mistresses, one of whom was an open secret and the other of whom was a deadly secret.

The one everyone knew about but pretended not to, was Elaine Dunne, the incredibly silly but attractive wife of one of Ireland 's leading broadcasters. Yes, the wife of dear Paddy Dunne, the nation's favourite TV host, was infatuated with the Minister for Justice, a man twice her age and twice as horrible as her husband.

I mean, Paddy Dunne is no prize but at least his teeth are his own. And while he throws the average number of tantrums you would expect from a television star, I never heard anything to suggest his temper was in Fitzpatrick's league.

Nevertheless, the lovely Elaine had been a regular in Damian's bed for the past year and seemed utterly besotted with him. She was notoriously indiscreet. I knew Mark Jacobs had been driven demented by her antics, showing up at all hours and waltzing in to see the Minister. In the previous year, I had become adept at keeping her name from even the most remote connection with Damian.

She acted as if she was terrified of her husband finding out but did everything short of ringing a radio show to confess. And she was terminally stupid. I once had a conversation with her about fake tan. Fifteen minutes of her talking to me about fake tan. Earnestly. I wanted to break my own arm just to relieve the tedium.

She rang my phone – my work land line thankfully, not my private number. It was 6.30 pm on the day after Damian had "shuffled off this mortal coil." I was already deep in funeral prospectuses and deciding what funeral home to go with, when an unknown number popped up on the screen. I answered expecting it to be Diffney's Discreet Undertakers or Fitzherbert's Family Funerals; instead, I got the breathy tones of Ireland's least faithful house-spouse.

"Caroline" she wailed, "Oh Caroline…"

Oh Christ.

I could barely understand her, she was gulping and sobbing so heavily. It was hard not to feel sorry for the poor cow – whatever her faults she seemed genuinely distraught at losing her beloved Damian. At least someone mourned him, I thought.

By dint of listening carefully I finally made out what she was saying

"I-I can't believe it. I can't. Oh god, what will I do?" - and sighed.

"Elaine, I'm terribly sorry but –"

"Why didn't you tell me? I heard it on the news! How could you be so heartless…"

"Eh, I only heard it myself moments before it was announced, Elaine. How could I possibly have told you?"

"You should have told me, I was his love, I was his little Bunny."

Oh, Good God. For a moment, I considered hitting myself in the face with a stapler just to get off the phone.

"You should have found a way…. have you any idea, any idea how it felt? Hearing it on the news, like I was nothing to him, nothing!" she hissed down the phone.

Ah here. I couldn't spend all evening on the phone listening to this.

"What do you mean, Elaine?"

Silence, suspiciously free of sobbing. In a much sharper tone she said, "What do you mean?"

"Well, I know you were friends, but why should you be told first? After all his wife and children are the most important people in all this, I'm sure you'd agree. Friends have to come second, with the best will in the world."

I could almost hear her brain creaking as she tried to catch up. Welcome to reality, Elaine. You may have been his little Bunny, but Margaret is his Widow and in dear old Ireland, Widows trump Tramps, every time.

Plus, without Damian, I suspected she wouldn't want to lose her husband just yet.

"Well, um, yes – obviously. But, Damian and I were especially friendly"

"I don't follow, sorry."

"Um. Damian and I – I mean, I would have thought someone would have told me…"

"We seem to be going around in circles, Elaine. I understand you're very upset – we all are. I'll pass your condolences onto his widow and family, shall I?"

Silence. "Um. Yes. Thanks."

Good gods in their heavens, spare me. Did she really think anyone was going to acknowledge her publicly as Damian's grieving bit on the side? I shrugged and got on with the business of arranging a state funeral. Or as Stephen insisted on calling it, the Semi-State Funeral.

It was a few days later that the other shoe dropped. The other, "Other Woman" (if you'll forgive the pun.) I was a little taken aback. We had bet on her remaining stoically silent but apparently, there was a chink in her armour. This was something Journalists would have found hard to believe. In fact, it did cross my mind that should all else fail, I could always sell the story to the papers.

There wasn't one who wouldn't pay good money for the story that our toughest politician, Minister for Education, loathed by one and all, had been merrily bedding the Justice Minister for the last five years.

Lillian Roche was in her late forties, a stern and ruthless woman. Her style was homely Donegal tweeds and sensible shoes, and clean living.

Only a handful of us, namely Mark, Damian's brother Liam and I, knew that she was a catalogue of kinky tastes with an insatiable sexual appetite.

At least that's what Damian insisted on confiding in us late one night while in a tired and emotional state. I shuddered to contemplate it to be honest. Because, I may have mentioned, she was scary.

Lillian had a permanently aggressive expression; what Paula's mother would have termed "a face like a bulldog licking piss off a nettle."

She looked as if she might devour her mate after sex and cuddling her could only be likened to snuggling up to an angry forward prop. Yet she had Damian eating out of the palm of her hand in a way that Elaine could never aspire to.

Damian wasn't renowned for his loyalty to anyone but in his own warped way he had been loyal to her.

Various political scandals had dogged Minister Roche – the exam papers for sale scandal in some of Ireland's top fee-paying schools or the sacking of a pregnant teacher by a catholic secondary. Despite the entire country pretty much agreeing she was incompetent, deluded and impossible, the Government hierarchy had stood by her, to a man.

From which I deduced that Damian hadn't been her only conquest.

Unlike Elaine Dunne, Minister Roche was a mistress of self-control. Literally. In the days following his death, Damian's secret lover never once so much as twitched an eyebrow despite giving many solemn interviews and sound bites on the sad loss of a valued colleague. Damian's brother Liam, who had been the Minister's sidekick, handed me a copy of the Irish Times with a sigh; there was a large spread featuring Lillian being interviewed about the possible candidates for Minister of Justice, discussing her deceased lover's replacements with no visible signs of trauma.

Liam was a nice man, whose only real fault had been throwing his lot in with his Machiavellian brother. He'd been abused and debased for most of his adult life. He once confided that if he had any other skill set, he would leave Damian's employ in the morning.

I hadn't had a chance to ask him yet what he was planning on doing now that the Minister was dead, but I had a couple of ideas of my own on that subject. Making a mental note to talk to Liam about ghost writers and a biography of his beloved brother, I moved on with my day. Until Lillian

Roche herself appeared in the Leinster house offices, moving purposefully towards me, with what a lesser woman might think was menace.

"Good morning, Minister," I smiled sweetly. "How can I help you?"

She grunted, her bony lined face a mask of disdain. "So, you're organizing this circus of a funeral then?"

Good god, the woman had no manners. The rules were, I could call it a circus of a funeral in the privacy of my own head. But it would be a different matter if half the Oireachteas was gossiping that I allowed Lillian to do so.

"I beg your pardon?"

She snorted and then with a pointed sneer, shut the door that separated my cubbyhole from the rest of the room and rolled her eyes.

"God you're such a crawler aren't you. Still licking up even though he's in his grave!"

"Actually, he's not in his grave Lillian, that's rather the point. Where I'm from, it's manners not to refer to the deceased's funeral as if it was an inconvenience."

I could tell she'd love to smack me. I swear I saw her fist clench and unclench in her lap. Stuff it, I thought. I may have to play nice most of the time with a bunch of appalling fools but no matter how much I try to get on with this one, she will never like me anyway - so I may as well be honest.

"Don't get smart with me." Her eyes fixed on mine in an attempt to intimidate me. It was a good attempt. "It's bad enough you've made me walk down here to find out what's happening. You couldn't be bothered coming to see me, could you?"

Holy god, did every woman Damian ever shagged expect me to contact her and give her a special role in the man's funeral?

"I don't understand your point, Minister Roche. Did your secretary not get a copy of the order of service?"

She snorted. "Don't speak to me like I was just another colleague of his. You know better than that."

Time to employ that hard neck and brazenness for which I am justly famed.

"Do I? I'm terribly sorry Minister but as far as I am aware, Minister Fitzpatrick held all his cabinet colleagues – indeed his fellow party members-in equal esteem."

He did, he thought they were all equally awful gobshites.

"Are you trying to rile me, girlie?" Minister Roche practically snarled, leaning forward across my desk. "Are you? Because I'm not in the mood to put up with it from a little bitch like you. You were Damian's lackey when he was alive and I'll bet you're Margaret's now, aren't you? Now, drop the playacting. You knew fine well about Damian and me. What the hell do you mean by not informing me of the funeral arrangements in person?"

"Only those directly involved in the service need one to one coaching, Minister. All you have to do is attend. I fail to see what exactly you wanted me to do? There is no need for you to know any part of the arrangements other than the time it starts, where you sit and whether the family want flowers."

I stood up. I can be quite impressive when I try, being almost 6 foot has its advantages at times. I extended my hand and finished, "I'm sure Mrs. Fitzpatrick and Damian's family will be touched that you stopped by personally, but there's no need for you to trouble yourself. The family have decided on everything, and as long as they're happy, I'm sure we all are. After all, they're the important ones, aren't they?"

Lillian's face turned a very unattractive shade of red and she actually shook with anger.

"How dare you" she hissed, but she stood up all the same. "You're a smart little cow aren't you!" was her parting shot as she stormed out.

So, sue me, I don't like women who sleep their way to power. Elaine Dunne might have been silly but at least she never took anything from Damian; there were a dozen better women than Roche who should have been in her place, doing a decent job and really achieving something.

I could open my door and see a dozen of them walking the corridors of power right now. And what I hated most of all, was that our Minister actively tried to exclude other women from power.

I believe in the Old Girls Network – the sisterhood, regardless of class, colour or creed. Regardless even of political differences, within reason. The Minister would go out of her way to do another woman a bad turn. Lillian

Roche was bitch.

And now she was a bitch who hated me. Some days you just can't get it right.

5

Chapter Five

"Therefore, since we have been justified by faith, we have peace with God through our Lord Jesus Christ, through whom we have gained access (by faith) to this grace in which we stand, and we boast in hope of the glory of God."

I closed my eyes and let the sound of Monsignor Flanagan soothe my frazzled nerves. No one delivered a funeral reading like the good Monsignor. I had planned on having the Taoiseach or one of the political big wigs read, but when Paula had suggested Flanagan it was a stroke of genius. If you are ever planning an important funeral – ah, you know what I mean, obviously, all funerals are important, yada yada, but a really important, public one -you can't go wrong if you have an Archbishop celebrating the mass and a Monsignor reading.

Flanagan was also not merely a Monsignor, but a leading advocate of civil rights, liberalism, reform of the church, and social justice. He was the one cleric I could stand. Damian's miserable, shriveled soul benefited by his mere presence. And our beloved Taoiseach didn't mind being seen in his company. It was still important to the party faithful in rural areas that their leader was a Catholic, but the more progressive types didn't want to see him standing next to a homophobic, woman hater either.

At first the Monsignor had been a little reluctant, but Paula's mother knew his mother and between them they arranged it. In return, I made Margaret give him a generous donation for his favorite charity. And Paula's mother gave his mother a precious cutting of her prize-winning rhododendron.

The venue was the Pro-Cathedral. It was a source of historic bitterness that Dublin boasted two magnificent, ancient cathedrals both of which had been seized by the Church of Ireland. The Catholic cathedral was a far less imposing building and was only the "acting" cathedral. I presume Catholics harboured dreams of one day reclaiming one of the real ones back.

As a card-carrying atheist, I couldn't care less. A humanist ceremony in an Eco-friendly coffin would do me when the time came.

But the interior was beautiful, especially the elaborately carved pews and the mosaic aisle. It was the best option available, so we took it. Now I was inside I was impressed. I haven't been to mass voluntarily since childhood but if I ever relapsed back into religion, I'll haunt the place.

All in all, it was going well. The family were troopers. Margaret of course did her weeping widow act, but in the circumstances, it was appropriate. The boys were genuinely distraught, you had to feel for them. I suppose whatever faults Damian had as a husband, politician, boss and generally as a human being, he had doted on the boys and their families.

I glanced at them; they were all very similar. Big, tall, well built, rugby loving men with high colour in their cheeks and sandy hair. They were all attractive enough in a generic way; none of them devastatingly handsome, none of them evil looking.

They were all married except the second youngest and best looking. That was Rory, I recalled. The others – David, Paul, Francis, and James – were all attached to nice looking women who were well groomed without being glamourous. I wondered how Margaret would have coped with a high maintenance daughter in law. Probably by stabbing her through the eye.

I hovered a discreet 4 rows back from the family, standing to one side of the aisle. The whole of the Pro-Cathedral was filled with the great and the good, but the first four rows boasted the greatest and most socially desirable.

O'Mahony, and the cabinet occupied a row. President Mac Aonghusa and her husband were guests of honour, on the family row. Behind them were clustered some of the opinion leaders and movers and shakers of Irish society. Once you left the warm rich glow of the front rows you met the second tier; extraordinarily rich builders and the horsey set sitting shoulder to shoulder with the It people and the Media stars.

I spied Patrick Gillespie, a man routinely referred to on news programs as Ireland's leading developer and by people who had dealing with him as Ireland's most brazen crook. He was accompanied by his wife, a hard-faced woman with bleached blonde hair.

They were seated in the middle, which was some achievement. Usually at events like this, the back rows were the social equivalent of the outer regions of Siberia but today even the worst pews were filled with important names and faces.

The Eulogy had proved to be tricky. Ideally from my point of view the bigger the name the better – I would have asked Barack Obama to pop over if I could (if only Damian had been from Offaly!) However, the family naturally wanted it to be one of the sons or a close relative. We suggested Liam, but in the end the eldest of the Fitzpatrick boys, David, took the lectern. He did a standard but sincere eulogy, about how lovely his dad was, how much they loved him – and he did it well. Actually, I had to admit it was the right choice, Damian's best trait was that he did love those boys. It was a nicely sincere touch.

Then the renowned writer Darby Little – poet, playwright, general pain in the hole – read one of his excruciating verses dedicated to the memory of "A great statesman." As usual he adopted a dirge-like drone quite unlike his real accent, that official "poetry reading" voice that always makes me want to scream. But it went down well with the congregation most of whom couldn't tell Yeats from a nursery rhyme but liked to feel they had been exposed to culture every now and then.

Finally, Catherine Thompson the soprano sang "Nearer my God to Thee" which compensated for the previous idiot. Glorious voice. And so, the service wound on, without any hitch, until the final "Go in Peace" and the undertakers moved in to quietly arrange Fitzpatrick boys as the pallbearers.

The family exited solemnly, Margaret flanked by daughters-in-law who fussed over her and tended to her with elaborate concern. I slipped out the side entrance and legged it round the front to oversee the transfer of coffin and mourners into cars – and found myself almost eye to eye with Detective Sergeant Doyle.

"Oh, ouch, sorry" I rubbed my elbow, having cracked it nicely off the wall, trying to avoid cannoning directly into him.

"Miss." God, he could make "good morning" sound like an accusation.

"Detective Sergeant," Two could play at laconic, so they could. I went to dodge around him, but he shifted very slightly barring my way. Over his shoulder, I could see the heads of mourners emerging from the church porch – I had to get out there.

"Sorry, I have to just get around you – I have to go help…"

He gave me another long, cold-eyed stare and then moved just enough to let me go by. My face went red for no reason other than that weird feeling you get when someone has treated you rudely, but you cannot for the life of you see why. "Thanks" I put as much sarcasm as possible into that one word then sped away.

Not a moment too soon as well; I caught one of the daughters-in-law clambering into the lead limousine and the driver of the third car turned out to be as deaf as a post, and not at all sure where the cemetery was. As ever after an Irish funeral, the mourners were happy to mill around and talk for half an hour. It had been the same the night before at the removal, only worse because they didn't have a burial to go to afterwards.

But at least it bought us some time to sort out who should be in which car and to nick a sat nav unit out of a journalist's van and install it in Gorgio's limo with the cemetery address keyed in.

When I say nicked, I mean I snuck through the line of cars until I spotted an unattended one and I hopped right in and stole it. I saw the journalist later at the funeral, huffing and puffing as he ran to catch up with the rest of us and it warmed the cockles of my heart.

Throughout all this I kept a weather eye on the crowd and now I knew what I was looking for, I spotted not only DS Doyle, but his older colleague and several other young men who could only be Gardaí. The Special Branch were, of course, out in force anyway but that's normal at an event like this.

Like traffic cops they're a necessary evil whenever more than one Minister gathers in the same place. But Doyle wasn't the usual Special Branch man; and neither, by the look of them, were his posse.

Then suddenly, as these things have a tendency to do, the crowd dispersed and the family sat into the cars, as the hearse engine started with a low purr. Once again, I had to race to my own car, which was parked ahead of the hearse. We had to get there before everyone else if only to beat the journalists back with a big stick.

Only when we had the mourners established by the freshly opened grave did I relax a little; there was still the official wake to go but the public part, the part I could be judged on, was almost over. Stephen and Paula were pale with exhaustion, I owed them a massive "thank you" drink. But we had done an amazing job, and whatever happened at least we would go out with a bang.

I tipped a nod in the direction of the coffin – "Goodbye you auld rip, it was a terrible but exciting four years. I just wish I'd saved my salary instead of spending it all. But who knew you'd die like that?" – and stepped back to allow the photographers take a few tasteful shots of the graveside.

"Dignified to the end," my internal editor decided.

The wake was to be held in Fitzpatrick's home (caterers had been there since dawn) so just before the funeral broke up completely, I touched Margaret's arm and whispered that I'd go ahead and get things set up. She turned towards me and grasped both my arms.

"Oh Caroline, dear, you're so good! What would we have done without you?" At least half a dozen people turned around to have a good look at us, and the rest were also looking but a little more discreetly. I kissed her warmly on her cheek. "You've been so brave, Margaret. Looking after these little things…it's the least I can do."

Mutual admiration ensued for a few moments until the next in line claimed her attention. I had to hand it to her, it was classy. She had done all she could to publicly acknowledge my work.

And now I was free to leave. Well, free to run to her house and make sure no one stole the silver or ate the good biscuits before the important guests arrived.

6

Chapter Six

DS Alan Doyle

My ex used to say she thought police officers going to the funeral was in extremely bad taste. She never understood that taking advantage of the raw moments was part of our job. If you can catch people at their more vulnerable times, you never knew what you might learn from them. And then there's the fact that funerals tend to bring together everyone in the victim's life. It was a unique opportunity to observe them.

Anyway, we were meant to attend funerals for Ministers and prominent figures. Which was handy seeing as we were still pretending Minister Fitzgerald wasn't a murder victim. Frankly, the politics of it all made my head hurt. We were all on edge – Graves told me over a pint that he had nightmares where he had to break the news to An Taoiseach and the man sacked him on the spot.

"Don't worry," I told him. "It's Looney who will have to tell him, and O'Mahony will sack all of us, including the Doc."

Doctor O'Toole was in a state of seething rage at us, bitterly regretting going against her better judgment. She rang Looney twice a day to yell at him, and when Locke emailed her asking questions about another case, her reply contained the words "I hate all of you."

At least the funeral gave us a chance to actually do something. A frisson of excitement ran through me as I watched the mourners file into the church.

There were the usual suspects all right, but here and there some anomalies. Patrick Gillespie, the crooked auld goat. Sitting there bold as brass. An odd bedfellow for the clean-cut Minister Fitzpatrick. Or was he here just to be social, to "pass himself" as my mother would say?

I watched the family carefully. It seemed highly unlikely considering he died at his desk, but you always have to consider the nearest and dearest. My first sergeant used to preach, it's always the ones you love that will pour bleach into your morning coffee.

Margaret Fitzpatrick was a well-preserved late fifties, brunette, still slim enough, and very well turned out. You didn't have to be a fashionista to recognize the cut and quality of her clothes. She looked somber but composed. Behind her trailed a parade of tall men, and well-groomed blonde women. Obviously, the sons had a type. Each wore expensive black jackets and coats, over navy or olive-green dresses. Each had their hair in neat twists, wore similar makeup, clutched interchangeable bags.

The sons shared Fitzpatrick's ruddy good looks; all bar the youngest had his sandy coloured hair. They trooped dutifully behind their mother, arranging themselves and their spouses in the first two rows. Only the younger son – Rory, I recalled the name – broke ranks, pausing to talk to some of the older people, pressing hands and exchanging a few words here or there.

He was the only one who had inherited anything in looks from Margaret. His hair was dark, his good looks a little more refined. He had the build of his siblings though. They were all well-built, rugby playing types.

From across the cathedral, I could see Graves and Powers, both casting an eye over the congregation. As the service wore on – the worst bit was a terrible poem by a shifty looking individual, looked the image of a bloke I nicked once for stealing underwear off a clothesline – I caught sight of Caroline Jordan. She seemed to be acting as a compere, or leader of ceremonies – you had to admire her brass neck, I suppose. I wondered if Margaret knew, or cared, about her husband's lovers over the years.

Pity he hadn't died at home, I thought, then she'd be a prime suspect. Nice and simple.

The service ended and the coffin was carried out by the sons, with two men I recognized as Liam Fitzgerald and Margaret Fitzpatrick's brother Karl. Karl was a musician of some note, a real star of traditional Irish music.

I worked my way around the church taking careful note of who exchanged words, who seemed intent on avoiding each other. Once the crowd thinned, I stepped out the main doors and turned towards the car park. A figure charged around the side of the church, from the side door and before I could react, Caroline Jordan more or less fell over my feet, a very unladylike and unsuitable expression escaping her lips.

"Miss," I said politely, managing to sound professional but friendly. Perhaps the best way with her would be to be a bit chummier, as Locke had slyly suggested. She was hardly my type, but she was undoubtedly an attractive woman. Her hair was shiny, in a way I associated with TV shows, not real life. She sported a full head of curly, dyed blonde hair that made her look chic and funky and must have been hell to maintain (my ex had curly hair, so I was well up on the trials and tribulations of frizz, gloss, tangles and so on.) She looked …sharp. Sharp and chic and slightly intimidating.

And the look she gave me was pure poison. You'd think I'd insulted her, instead of stopped her falling on her face. I also couldn't help noticing in the very few, terse words we exchanged that she was not happy to see me there. She legged it around me like a scalded cat.

I was tempted to follow her, just to see what was so important but as I turned, I found myself staring into the face of Mark Jacobs.

The civil servant looked drawn and pale. Hardly upset at his boss' demise, from all I had gathered so far. Still, I could be doing him an injustice. Some people hated funerals, even if they weren't close to the departed.

"Garda," He gave me a nod of greeting.

"Mr. Jacobs." I glanced around. "A huge turnout."

"Yes. Yes, of course. Well, he was very well known, a major figure."

I noticed he didn't say "very well liked."

"Of course," I agreed. "Still, quite some range of characters here, isn't there?" I gestured to a group nearby, where Patrick Gillespie was talking loudly to, or rather at, several politicians and their wives. It was hard to tell whether they were listening out of politeness or because they were afraid to move away.

A frown crossed Jacobs' face. "That man." His tone was one of loathing, well beyond mere dislike. "I'm surprised he had the nerve to attend."

"Oh? I suppose he was friendly with the deceased…"

"Friendly! He is a snake, Detective, and it's a disgrace that he's not in a prison cell somewhere. You know it as well as I do."

He shook his head, and I was struck again by how tired he looked.

"Never mind me. I used to be in Environment, and I saw first-hand what the Gillespies of this world can do. He's rotten to the core." He stalked off, without another word.

File that under "Interesting" I told myself.

Looney had drawn the line at us attending the wake itself, although the Garda Commissioner would be putting in an appearance. It meant we had a very small window to observe the family and mourners. With that in mind I maneuvered myself as close to the family party as possible at the graveside. I was pressed between an elderly couple who kept passing rather loud remarks to each other about neighbouring gravestones ("oh look, Paudie, that poor woman was only 42…") and an elegant couple in their late thirties, friends of one of the sons from what they said.

"Rory looks so sad," the woman whispered to her companion. He nodded, adding "He was awful close to his dad, especially this new project he was starting. Rory was full of it a few weeks ago, how successful it was going to be…He was so proud to be working with the old man."

"So sad," she murmured before the decade of the rosary started.

I itched to know what project exactly, but a direct question would hardly be diplomatic right now. I wished Locke were here, he'd be on first name terms with the couple in two minutes, with all the gossip.

7

Chapter Seven

Caroline Jordan

The wake was in full swing. I was wrestling a platter of crab and lobster from a stubborn waiter when Mark Jacobs appeared at my elbow'. He whispered, "Come outside, out the front!" in my ear and just as quickly, disappeared.

It was at least a quarter of an hour before I could get away, to find him waiting for me in the front garden. Before I could say anything, he grabbed my arm and gave it a warning squeeze.

"Ah Caroline, I was just about to go…." He muttered clichés at me about the sadness of the occasion as he propelled me out the gate and halfway down the road. Away from curious listeners. Ever the professional, I thought.

I could see his car parked a few metres away. Mark sighed, looked around him and said, rather inconsequentially, "That house gives me the willies, you know that? Like a mausoleum already. She'll have a shrine up by the end of the month."

I laughed but I was impatient. I was very fond of Mark, really, and his sardonic humour had saved my sanity many a day, but this wasn't the place for it.

"Yeah, well, I suppose it's hard on the family," I said. Mark shot me a look.

"Yeah, I suppose," he said, "I suppose."

We stood there in awkward silence, him staring into space and me wondering whether the catering staff were drinking all the wine in the kitchen. I was itching to get back inside. Mark on the other hand, seemed to be intent on staging a freaking Beckett play on the street.

"What do you think of it all, Caro?" His sensitive, clever face was drawn and tired looking. He glanced at his hands and then at my feet and then – fixing his gaze somewhere between the lamp post and the nearest hedgerow - "I'm worried about it all, to be honest."

I choked back my initial, bitter response – seriously, as a senior civil servant, Mark had no reason to worry, his job was safer than a Ministers! But he was a good mate, and he looked worried – it wouldn't kill me to be a bit less selfish.

"Don't worry," I said, "Sure, you'll be fine. No one could be much worse than Damian and whoever gets the Ministry, you'll have them in shape in no time. Pity your poor untenured colleagues instead. I'm the one who will be begging on Grafton Street in a month."

He sighed. "No. No I mean…" He shrugged. "I don't know what I mean."

He sounded so worried; I took a proper look at him. "Is anything wrong, Mark? What's up?"

He shrugged. "Nothing. No really, nothing. I'm just being silly. Honestly." He seemed to realize how unconvincing he sounded, and he laughed ruefully.

When he spoke again, he sounded far more like the Mark I knew. "Ah here, listen to me. I'm like an old lady whining about how times are changing. I'm getting old, Caroline. I guess I just don't like having to train in a new one, eh?"

I smiled. "You are getting old! You should find yourself a nice boy and settle down, someone to come home to of an evening. Save you running around all those trendy bars trying to look cool."

Mark was a very popular lad, never had any trouble pulling. Most of his boyfriends were a bit younger, none of them lasted long. Same as myself, really.

"Bitch. Ah maybe you're right. I could do with a love life. I'm tired of being alone at funerals and weddings." He suddenly laughed. "Oh! Sorry, I'm keeping you away from the production in there, aren't I? Great job by the way."

He fished about in his pockets and pulled out an envelope, a small, padded jiffy bag one.

"Actually, can I ask you a massive favour? I meant to ask before but…well, with everything that's been going on it slipped my mind. I've a few short stories I wrote, I did them on the PC in the office over the last few months."

Only his best friend Gerry and I knew that Mark wrote, he'd already had a few short stories published, and we were used to proof reading and critiquing them for him. He rarely wrote at home – despite being in his thirties, he shared a house with two very noisy, boisterous sisters from Roscommon. He seemed fond of them, but personally I would have strangled them in their sleep. I could easily believe that the atmosphere wasn't conducive to quiet creativity.

"I deleted them off the PC and saved them on a drive, but of course I've been carrying it around with me ever since. I want to go over them again at some point, but would you mind holding on to a copy of them for me?"

"Sure. Want me to cast an eye over them?"

"No. No please, not yet." He looked at me and smiled again. "I know I can trust you, Caro. I'd like to work on them a bit more, OK? But I don't want them on the work PC with all the upheavals in the office."

"Grand," I said. I stuffed it into the pocket of my coat and kissed his cheek. "I hate to run, Mark but I have to get back in. Take care of yourself, OK? And give me a ring when you're free for lunch!"

"I'll keep my ear to the ground for you," he volunteered, "if there's anything in your line?"

"Oh do, thanks" He really was a pet, I'd miss working closely with him. And if I didn't get back into the funeral, I might not be working with anyone, I chided myself.

8

Chapter Eight

The day of Derek's funeral was the longest in living memory. By the time the last important guest left I was in a fugue of exhaustion. Even then I couldn't relax and just bugger off. It takes delicate navigation to extricate yourself from a personal tragedy that you have infiltrated for mercenary gain. I gathered the troops, and we inched our way to freedom, smiling and nodding all the way.

Several long hours later Stephen, Paula and I were ensconced in the pub getting as drunk as three exhausted, underfed people can get after a day of manic activity. Which as it turns out was very drunk indeed.

Stephen was inclined to be pessimistic – as the last person hired, he assumed he'd be let go first, he said. And, honestly, he would be so sorry to leave us, but he wouldn't blame me. Not at all, I assured him, if we go bust, we all go together.

"What are our chances?" Paula asked wincing.

"All things considered; we are not completely screwed. Not yet. We still have the Women in Need charity, the Cat's Paw charity ball, and the Best Buy chain store. There are a lot of other small contracts. Without Damian, things will be tough, though. God knows that man bankrolled us through the lean months. If I can land us another political contract, or even some more large charity ones, over the next couple of months – we'll be fine."

"Fingers crossed then" Stephen said rather gloomily. Paula gave him a playful slap.

"It'll be fine. Caroline always come through for us."

While I was touched, I couldn't help feeling her trust might be misplaced. For a week, I'd thrown myself into organizing the funeral, as if that alone would save us, but here we were, Damian safely buried, and no replacement employment in sight.

I tried to tell myself that I was being paranoid and worrying unnecessarily and that it was far too early to panic but later that night I awoke from a nightmare in a cold sweat. I had dreamed about walking into Diva's nightclub, the venue of choice for the Irish Glitterati and some clipboard Nazi had stepped out of the shadows screeching "You're not on the list! You're not on the list!" while various socialites and media types howled with laughter and pointed at me.

Things would be vastly different if we didn't hustle up some work.

For a week, all was quiet. October moved into November, and we picked up some smaller contracts all right. I was kept busy working on the board of "Cats Paw." This is the charity for abandoned cats run by the charming but batty Anglo-Irish Lady Foxrock. 80 years old and obsessed with cat welfare.

Yes, her name had a certain cachet, but I still felt uneasy – it was all a bit scrappy and lacked the security of working as Damian Fitzpatrick's personal PR adviser.

With the Recession, Stephen opined, there's no budget for extras like press advisers and public relations, and I was half afraid he was right. Although without us the political system would be boring, and politicians would look uglier.

"We must diversify," Paula said sternly. "There's always a way if we only look hard enough. We should try to think outside the box – what other types of work should we be bidding for? That kind of thing."

"I'm only fit for this," I said, "My skill set is viciously limited."

Week two started badly; I had to deal with a very neurotic marketing manager from Best Buy, one of those men who constantly micromanage. A complete control freak, Paula called him. He fretted and double checked everything, then complained, and fretted and triple checked everything.

That would be fine – perfectionists are not a problem. But then he would completely forget what was agreed, and swear blind it was our mistake, not his.

That was the problem.

My blood pressure was about to go through the roof when he finally settled on one of the proposals for an in-store promotion and took his leave. He would ring as soon as he got back to Best Buy headquarters, to go over it all one more time, but at least I had a breather for half an hour.

He was a classic example of someone promoted beyond their capabilities. Not my favourite type of person. I deeply resented every time I'd been patronized or passed over on the grounds that I was a woman. Then some twit like him would get the gig.

In a thoroughly bad temper, I stalked around the office – tiny but very nicely decorated, not a tempted maiden in sight – and looked for something decent to eat.

"Why are there only crappy plain biscuits in the cupboard?"

Paula looked up from her computer and said calmly "Stephen bought them. He says we should try to cut costs and that no one needs chocolate biscuits."

"I do." It was raining out. There was no way I wanted to go out into the cold and the wet just to get some flaming biscuits. "I'm going out to get some flaming biscuits."

"Good for you," Paula said. "Bring us back a Twix, will you? And a Bounty for Steve."

I sometimes suspected that Paula was secretly mad about Stephen, the way she looked after him. Like, it's fair enough she makes me a cup of coffee every morning, as I am her boss and best friend. But she makes him special, twice-the-price-of normal-coffee de-caff coffee because he had to give up caffeine but bemoaned the fact that he missed the taste.

Grumbling like a child I stalked off to the shops. I returned in an absolutely foul mood, having been rained on, jostled, and made wait while the checkout girl answered her mobile. As a final insult I was splashed by a passing taxi just as I got back to our office block.

I burst into the foyer of our little firm's office suite, frothing at the mouth.

"The stinking brain-dead twats out there," I began.

Paula appeared from behind the reception desk waving both hands frantically at me and mouthing "O'Mahony! Michael T O'Mahony!" Just in time as it happened, because the words frozen on my lips were not those suitable for the ears of a carefully nurtured Taoiseach.

With a superhuman effort, I rearranged my face into a pleasant, calm expression, stuffed a mint Aero, a Twix and a Bounty back into the pocket of my coat and floated into the main office space. Michael T was sitting on our good chair, being plied with tea and biscuits by Stephen, while holding forth on the evils of Dublin traffic.

"Taoiseach!" I managed a credible moment of happy surprise and extended both hands to the nation's premier. "How lovely to see you!"

"Ah Caroline," he beamed at me. Stephen had obviously put him in high good humour. He put down his biscuit (good ones, I noticed sourly. Chocolate ones. They'd been holding out on me.) He took both my hands in his. "It's great to see you, you're looking very well!"

"Why thank you," I gave him my bright and youthful smile, the one most male politicians like best and said, "What brings you to us in that weather?"

"Ah, now…" Michael assumed a serious mien. "I've come to talk to you, Caroline, so I have."

My mercenary little heart beat faster. "Won't you step into my office?" I waved him into the tiny inner sanctum of Jordan PR and closed the door on the other pair. I eased myself into the nearest chair and insisted he take the larger, "good" seat. Deference can be shown in many subtle ways.

"Well now," O'Mahony smiled his famous Man of the People" smile. "You did poor Damian proud with that funeral."

Cue a modest murmur along the lines of "least I could do" and "poor dear Damian."

He waved aside my protestations and said "Credit where it's due, Caroline. I wouldn't mind a send-off like that myself when my time comes. And you certainly ah, put Damian's best side forward, eh? Very good. Very good indeed. So, now what?"

Now what, indeed.

"Well, of course, it's been a big change." I looked at him in an earnest and honest manner.

"Not a bad change in some ways, to be honest. Jordan PR is my brainchild, my baby. It's been good to be more hands-on these last few weeks. We have a lot of clients at the moment, all wanting the personal touch and of course with Christmas coming…. lots to do. And of course, Cats Paw…."

I gave it the same reverent tones some people use when saying "Band Aid."

"It's a cause so dear to my heart, and dear Lady Foxrock relies on us so much." No need to tell him that I loathed cats. I couldn't help it, my mother had Ailurophobia and while I wasn't quite as bad, she had passed on a deep mistrust of the moggy. About the only thing she gave me without strings attached.

O'Mahony nodded gravely. "I can imagine. Lady Foxrock, eh? I must look in at that. But say an offer was forthcoming, I take it you're not dead set against coming back into the political arena?"

Yes!

"Back? You mean, working for some Minister or other? I suppose – well, I don't know. Damian Fitzpatrick wasn't exactly an easy man to work for, but it was so interesting. When you've worked for someone like that, it's hard to imagine doing the humdrum sort of stuff."

In other words, I'll do anything, please hire me. I hoped my face was carefully neutral but O'Mahony definitely had a twinkle in his eye as he digested that piece of bullshit.

"Well, now. I flatter myself that I can offer you a challenge. I don't think the office of An Taoiseach could be described as humdrum, exactly."

He smiled that smile again.

"Let me be frank. I have never liked using a large, impersonal firm for these things. I value…personality. Individuality. And I have been fortunate in my advisors. I don't mind saying I owe a great deal to Derek Fields, more than you know. And now…well, between us, Caroline, he is thinking of retiring. Not today or tomorrow but in a year or so, you understand. He is anxious to find a suitable protégée to train in. Frankly, he wants you. And I agree. I can't think of a better person to fill his shoes."

Derek Fields, the God of Media was retiring? The Duke of Leinster? I almost choked. He'd ruled O'Mahony's career for twenty years, I don't think Michael T. had given an interview or bought a shirt and tie in thirty years without consulting Fields.

I had been hoping for a humble PR role. He wanted me to take over Field's position? Derek Fields knows who I am? The little voice of reason in my head screamed "Stop thinking, say yes. Please, for the sake of Jordan PR, Paula and Stephen and your mortgage, say yes!"

I nearly broke my tongue getting the words out.

"Taoiseach! I-I don't know what to say – except of course that I'd be delighted. Working with you, that would be the absolute pinnacle. There's nothing I would rather than to take on that role."

Working with Derek Fields was the real prize though.

Michael T gave a contented grunt. "Ah now that's great." He really did manage to convey a warm and humble persona, as if my accepting his job offer brought him genuine pleasure.

"I don't mind telling you, since Derek told me he wanted to retire I've been dreading trying to replace him. It's not anyone could do Derek's job, it's a special position. It has to be someone with intelligence and sensitivity – and balls."

He gave a rueful chuckle. "I admired the way you handled Lillian. She's a great woman but Jaysus, she can be terribly difficult at times. I liked the way you protected Damian's reputation, even in death. And of course, poor Margaret. She raved about you, absolutely raved. Said she'd have been lost. Imagine her having to deal with Lillian, or Elaine, eh?"

There really were no secrets in politics, I reflected.

"That kind of loyalty impresses me, Caroline. Plus, you know how things work, but you're a little outside the system. Derek started out like that; you know. No, I said to myself at poor Damian's funeral, that's the ticket. Get Caroline Jordan on board now while Derek's still around and can bring you up to speed."

He gave a small sigh that suggested he really was relieved to have it sorted. "Derek will be in touch as soon as he's back from – he'll be delighted you accepted. Hammer it all with him, and start with us as soon as possible, if that's OK?"

OK? I practically threw rose petals in front of him as he exited. Judging from the pink excited faces on the other pair, they had had their ears glued to the door for the entire conversation. Stephen produced an umbrella out of thin air, a nice black one with a proper wooden handle, and carefully shielded An Taoiseach from the elements as he swept out to his waiting car. Royalty couldn't have been treated with more deference.

Once the sleek black limo had pulled away and we were safely back inside, the three of us shrieked like banshees and danced around the office.

"Oh my god. Oh my god," Paula said gasping "I can't believe it. Jordan PR, advisers to the Prime Minister, gurus of the political world. Caroline, you're a – you're a kingmaker now!" Kingmaker was Derek Fields unofficial title, considering he had steered an unremarkable looking candidate from council seat to head of government.

"Ah for the love of Mike, I'm a long way from that yet."

"You're a baby kingmaker then," Stephen gloated.

"Where are the biscuits? Where's the chocolates?" Paula demanded. "I need something for the shock and awe."

"Stuff the biscuits." I said grandly. "Let's go for a long, decadent, liquid lunch." Although I made a mental note to get my own back for them hiding the biscuits.

9

Chapter Nine

DS Doyle

The funeral hadn't yielded much. Still though, between Mark Jacobs and various bits of gossip, I felt it hadn't been a wasted trip.

None of my colleagues shared my upbeat mood. "A total stinking waste of time," Powers said disgustedly. "Standing there looking at a bunch of stuffed shirts, pretending not to work a case we are pretending isn't happening." He threw his jacket on his chair and ruffled his hair.

"I'm sick of it. Looney is insane, he should have just bitten the bullet."

Graves was of much the same mind. "I know, I know," he said, "Looney panicked in my opinion. We're doing our best but it's a ridiculous situation. We need to make something happen if we can't question people openly. We need to force the issue."

MacPherson was curious. "What had you in mind?"

Graves shrugged, "I'm not sure, but...we need to rattle cages. We need a pretext to start investigating. Like, say we hadn't copped there was something wrong. Say we were approached after the fact, after the burial, by someone stating they feared there had been foul play. What would we have done?"

Powers sat down and looked hard at Graves. "And if someone was to come forward even now..."

"Or, if there was enough rumour that we could make a case for investigating, set the public mind at rest..." Graves smiled, a great big full toothed gravestone smile.

"What about a little from column A and a little from column B?" Graves had the slightly constipated look he always gets when an idea is pushing its way through the fog in his brain.

"What I mean is…the one advantage we have is that we know it wasn't natural. The disadvantage is that we have too many suspects, no clear motive, no idea why or who. Can we use the one to shake out some facts about the other?"

I thought for a moment.

"You mean – what exactly?" I couldn't quite see how it would work.

"What about a whispering campaign? We let a few people know we think there is something wrong. Or we start a rumour. Once the rumour gets back to the people we can't touch, let's see what they actually do?"

McPherson sighed. "It's so random though. How can you possibly be sure it'll get back to the right people?"

"We can get at a few of Fitzpatrick' old friends – they'll make sure it gets back to the family."

"Do we suspect the family?"

"Oh Christ, it would be brilliant it turned out to be family," Locke said with a heartfelt sigh. Which was callous but accurate – a Minister bumped off by a disgruntled wife was a lot better than the prospect of having to arrest the leader of the country or the new Minister for Justice.

"We need a way to plant it right in the heart of the political crew though."

"Caroline Jordan." Graves tapped the folder in front of him and pointed to her name "She's got an alibi – she was definitely out of the building before Fitzpatrick died and she spent the next two hours at a fashion launch in Brown Thomas. In a land of no alibis, she is the nearest to clean we have got."

"Pity." I couldn't help it, I really thought she might have been a contender. She was hard-nosed, had been sleeping with the deceased and yet barely liked him, from all accounts. I could have made a case for her. "So how do we go about it?"

"Drop this in her lap and it'll be all around the Dáil by the weekend."

I nodded slowly, the idea taking hold. "Okay, so we start the rumour mill, behind Looney's back. We shake as many trees as possible, and we make people talk. Then we open an investigation, maybe even get someone higher up the food chain to demand one…"

"And no one has to explain to the Government that we covered up a Minister's murder because the prime suspects included a high-ranking politician and the leader of the country."

MacPherson was not convinced. "It's all a bit…. haphazard. It could backfire. And how are you going to start a rumour anyway? You can't exactly sidle up to a journo and start muttering about foul play."

"No…" Locke interjected, "But we all know who could! All we need to do is give that PR one a hint of scandal and it'll be all over Dublin by the weekend."

"Genius." Graves rubbed his hands together. "OK, we need to really get under her skin, make her convinced there's something going on."

He eyed me slyly. "We need someone with no bedside manner, who can look constantly suspicious. Someone who would make an angel feel guilty."

A unanimous chorus from my colleagues. "Doyle it is, then."

I think it was pure malice that made Graves suggest me as the person to approach her.

"You don't have to be polite," he said encouragingly, "Just be yourself."

10

Chapter Ten

Caroline Jordan

"Caroline."

Derek Fields' distinctive grumble was even more pronounced over the telephone. "Michael tells me you are coming on board with us. I'm delighted - I really am."

He sounded sincere but then again, he was a past master of faking sincerity. I had spent the intervening days since Michael T's visit researching everything about the man while wondering would the job materialize. Once the euphoria wore off as usual the worry set in; it seemed far too good to be true.

Even that morning waiting to see if Fields would ring had made me sick with nerves. I knew from the papers that he would be back from Helsinki the previous day and counted the minutes since. Yet, now here he was, and it seemed it was happening, I didn't know whether to weep with relief or puke with fright.

This was a major step up, even from being Minister Fitzpatrick's go-to girl. This was serious political influence. Okay, so I was pretty damn good at politics and no one could work a media event like I could – but still. This was major.

That horrible voice we all keep in our heads whispered that I was about to be found out. I was out of my depth. I could not fake my way through this. I pushed it down. It was wrong.

I could fake my way through anything.

"I think the best thing is for you to join us as soon as you possibly can; I don't intend on going anywhere just yet, but I want you embedded in the inner circle. In three months, we should be facing into a general election, an election I intend for us to win. So, you'll have to come up to speed quickly."

"I'll do it." I swallowed. Fingers crossed.

"You managed Damian Fitzpatrick beautifully over the last four years, I foresee no problems for you where Michael T is concerned."

Christ almighty, Derek Fields just complimented me. I forced myself to listen rather than dance around the office screeching.

"Mainly, you'll need to familiarize yourself with the ethos of Michael's politics. He has a very strong public persona, and an image that has taken years of hard work to build. That's sacrosanct."

"By all means update him; bring him into touch with the younger voter but above all he's a serious, respected politician and the leader of this country. There are certain events he must do and some he can't do under any circumstances, but you'll be familiar with that from Damian's office. Oh, that reminds me..."

I could hear the shuffling of papers on his desk. "There's going to be an announcement about the new Minister for Justice tomorrow, I thought you'd like to know."

For some reason I realized whose name he was going to say, a split second before he actually said it.

"Minister Roche will be leaving Education and entering Justice...."

I fecking knew it. At some cellular level, I just knew it.

"This is going to be a major media event, as you can imagine," he continued briskly. "I thought it would be an ideal time for you to come on board and see how these things work from this side, if it's not too short notice?"

It struck me that the great Derek Fields was being extremely gracious and accommodating; in return I decided on honesty.

"Derek, I won't lie to you. The opportunity to work with Michael T O'Mahony and the office of An Taoiseach, and especially, with yourself, is my top priority. I've off-loaded everything else to my staff so I can start whenever you want me."

There was a moment of silence followed by a small chuckle. "I appreciate that. I also appreciate you not giving me crap about finishing up big contracts and playing hard to get. Michael said you were straight – I'm very glad to see he was right. Come in tomorrow, early start. You'll be trailing me around for a while, but I promise it won't be boring."

I put down the phone feeling strangely elated. In my chosen profession, shallowness was a virtue on a par with godliness; it was easy to forget that there were serious people out there. The chance to do more than even Damian had offered – to work on really important political events, be the confidante of a party leader and prime minister, deal with the media on serious issues not just try to keep some Minister's girlfriend out of gossip columns - was a chance in a million.

"You did more than keep Elaine Dunne's name out of the papers, in fairness," Paula said indignantly when I told her my thoughts. "You did an amazing job for that man. You kept his good side in the public view, and you forced him to take a position on all kinds of things that he would never have given a moment's thought to, selfish old pig!"

"I think they're lucky to get you," Stephen added loyally and was rewarded with a beaming smile from Paula. He went red and returned to his pile of press cuttings and magazines. Once again, I made a mental note to ask Paula what the story was – not that I had the slightest objection as long as they both stayed with Jordan PR.

"Ah in all honesty, while working for Damian wasn't exactly on a par with planning supermarket openings for a pop star, it wasn't a patch on what Michael T wants either. One is, well, normal PR and media work. This is – well, it's more than that, it's being part of the inner circle, it's serious and important."

Paula looked at me anxiously. "Caroline, no offense but the last time you said something was important. it turned out to be the kitchen ware sale at Brown Thomas. You always say, don't swallow their bullshit. They're all the same, whether they're socialites and Irish Models or politicians and business people, that's what you always say."

"I know, I know, and I am aware that I sound like a star struck girlie but if media, PR, whatever you want to call it, has a serious side, this is it. I'll be making decisions about the leader of this country's public image. That's – that's worth doing," I finished lamely.

The worst thing was, I was serious.

11

Chapter Eleven

Ah here.

You'd think nothing much could go wrong between the day my job offer was made official and the next morning but hey, life has a habit of surprising us. I left work early – shamelessly early, blowing off a meeting with Mr. Best Buy the world's most neurotic, incapable marketing manager. The plan was to go shopping, go home, get a takeaway, do a some more swotting on Michael T O'Mahony and his cohorts. Then have a bath and an early night.

Everything went according to plan until my takeaway arrived – I always order from the same local Indian in Ranelagh. It's shameful to admit but they have my order on speed-dial. A nice boy called Giri usually brings it, a very obliging soul. As I live in an apartment block, he usually rings to tell me he was on his way, so I can get downstairs and collect it without having to break my neck hurrying.

Tonight, however I was caught by surprise – the buzzer went ten minutes earlier than expected and a voice said something that I presumed was "Takeaway."

"I'll buzz the door" I grabbed my purse and legged it; at least Giri could wait in the foyer, out of the cold.

I trotted into the apartment block foyer, my slippers making an oddly comic slapping sound against the marble floor. Giri was used to me

56

appearing in a variety of startling costumes, from full ballgowns to pajamas with an overcoat thrown on. You never know when you will need a takeaway.

"Giri," I started, then my brain caught up with my mouth.

It wasn't Giri, but Detective Sergeant Doyle, cold blue eyes and all.

"Oh." I looked at him in confusion. Where the hell was my lovely Indian man with my lovely Indian meal? Doyle cast a disparaging look over my garb – sweatshirt, leggings and slippers, hair tied up, face embarrassingly free of make-up – and said, "Is there some reason why you didn't want me to come to your door, Miss Jordan?"

"What?" Eejit! He thought I had known it was him over the intercom and had refused to let a respected member of an Garda Siochána call to my door.

"Eh, I thought you were my Indian." This didn't seem to clear any confusion, so I elaborated. "I ordered a takeaway, all I could hear over the intercom was a garbled message, I assumed it was my food arriving, I came down to pay."

He gave me a look that said "fool."

"Right. Well, as I said over the intercom, I would appreciate a few minutes of your time. Upstairs," he said pointedly. "I would like to speak to you in private."

Totally thrown off balance, I looked around me and hesitated.

"Um. Well, that's fine but I'm just waiting for my food…"

He looked at me incredulously. Bugger him, I was starving, and it was cold and what was the point of going back upstairs only to have to come down again in a couple of minutes when Giri arrived?

"If you don't mind waiting until my takeaway arrives, I can certainly give you a few minutes." I said firmly, trying to muster a little dignity. "But if that's inconvenient, perhaps another time?"

He narrowed his eyes. "No, I'd prefer to talk to you tonight. I suppose we can wait for this takeaway to arrive." He managed to imply that the takeaway was a fiction I'd invented solely to annoy him, and that he'd relish waiting here while it failed to materialize.

"Well, you can always tell me what you want while we're waiting," I snapped. "There's no one around so I'm sure it qualifies as private enough for anything you can possibly have to say?"

In response he gave a pointed look at the CCTV camera mounted in one corner. I nearly thumped him in exasperation. Like there was anything he could possibly have to say so important that a record of it on a crappy CCTV tape was remotely important.

I rolled my eyes – normally I'm perfectly polite to police officers, I'm inclined by nature to be on the side of Law and Order – but something about the smug-faced git rubbed me up the wrong way. Thankfully before I could ruin my political career by smacking a Garda, a cheerful voice called out "Ms. Jordan" and Giri, God bless him, appeared at the door waving.

Doyle watched in sullen silence as I paid for the food and exchanged pleasantries. His animosity was so evident that Giri said to me, his eyes fixed on Doyle "Are you alright, Ms. Jordan? Should I stay?"

"Thanks, Giri!" Really, he was such a sweetie. "But it's okay."

Some imp prompted me to add "This is a Detective Sergeant, Giri, A Garda. Police officer. Detective Sergeant Doyle."

Giri's face cleared. "Oh, very good. That's all right, eh?"

I didn't concur but at least someone now knew Doyle was visiting me late on a Thursday evening and that made me feel better for some reason. Doyle looked thunderous but said nothing, merely stalked upstairs beside me in silence. He stood in the middle of my living room staring around him with undisguised curiosity while I busied myself emptying my takeaway onto a plate.

Well, okay, I emptied half the takeaway out as if I were one of those dainty girls who wouldn't dream of stuffing an entire Lamb Korma and pilau rice into her face. I put the rest firmly in the fridge and strode to the tiny table.

Doyle waited until I was sitting down, and had a mouthful of food in my gob before saying "So, you're jumping into bed with O'Mahony now, are you?"

Choking I tried not to literally spit the food at him as I spluttered "What the giddy feck? What did you just say?"

Doyle raised one eyebrow and sneered. "I beg your pardon, I phrased that badly." Somehow, he made that sound like "na nah, na naaa na."

"Yes," I said icily. "You phrased that extremely badly. Is it possible that you could express yourself with a little less disrespect? What exactly are you asking me?"

To my surprise I was rewarded by a tiny flicker of embarrassment across that smug façade. He cleared his throat and looking anywhere but directly at me, said in a far politer tone of voice,

"Sorry. What I meant to say was, I understand you are about to join Michael T O'Mahony's staff. As next in line to Derek Fields if I've been correctly informed."

My head spun slightly. No official announcement had been made to the best of my knowledge and I had been far too paranoid about it all going belly-up to even consider telling anyone outside of Jordan PR. Even my mother didn't know. And believe me I would enjoy rubbing it in her face. She thought my career was a laughable triviality.

So, while it wasn't a secret exactly, it just wasn't common knowledge beyond a very select group of people and why on earth anyone who might have known would have bothered telling DS Doyle – and why DS Doyle would be remotely interested - was beyond me.

For a wild moment I considered denying just to see what he would say but I settled for "So?" which while not a sterling example of my wit and repartee at least bought me time to think.

"So, it's true?" He sniffed. I couldn't help but feel it was a disparaging sniff. "That's some gig, isn't it?

When I didn't respond, he continued, "Second in command to Derek Fields? Heir apparent to him, I should say. Quite a leap from being Damian Fitzpatrick's PR girl."

If the man had any point in mind other than annoying me, I failed to see it.

"Detective, I don't know if you have the faintest idea what the term "public relations" actually covers but where Minister Fitzpatrick was concerned, I had responsibility for presenting serious and important issues to the scrutiny of public opinion."

It might sound like I was quoting from my own CV but at least it was more dignified that "Eff off with yourself."

"While my new role will obviously be somewhat different, it is a natural progression for someone who has worked closely with a senior Minister of State."

That sounded good, and a lot more confident than I felt. Doyle shrugged. "No need to be defensive."

He leaned back against my breakfast counter and smiled. "I seem to be rubbing you up the wrong way, Miss Jordan. So, you will be joining the office of An Taoiseach tomorrow morning?"

Sister Assumpta.

My erratic memory threw up the comparison and I almost spat out the name. It was just like being sneered at by Sister Assumpta. She had been the "uniform nun" in my school, her job being to prevent any outbreak of individuality among the gabardine wearing unfortunates forced to attend the Blessed Virgin of the Bleeding Heart secondary school.

She used to catch me at every opportunity – skirt too long, skirt too short, tie not straight, no tie, and on one memorable occasion, purple hair – and her greatest pleasure seemed to be recounting a litany of my every shortcoming and predicting a swift and inglorious end to my pathetic life. Doyle had the same eyes and it seemed, roughly the same opinion of me. In fact, stick a wimple and habit on him and it could be her.

But I had survived Sr Assumpta and I would be damned if some narky cop was going to speak to me like that.

I lowered my fork, placing it deliberately on the table and stared straight at him, in complete silence. He remained slouched and smiling until it dawned on him that the silence had stretched far beyond anything comfortable. Staring at a point just above his head I relaxed and waited.

He straightened up, fidgeted, coughed. I stared. He hummed and hawed and then ploughed on with "I'm not asking out of idle curiosity, Miss Jordan."

"Detective, I have no idea why you are here, or why you are interested in my career choices. I am however intrigued by your manner and at a loss to explain your rudeness. If you have anything to say to me, any reason at all for this visit, I suggest you spit it out or leave."

God bless you Sr. Assumpta, I hated your guts, but you gave me balls of steel and a resistance to interrogation that the CIA would envy.

Doyle coloured. "Obviously, I wouldn't disturb you at home without a good reason," he said stiffly. "This is a delicate situation."

Delicate? And they had no gorillas they could send instead of Doyle?

"I must ask you to keep both this visit and the subject of this discussion private."

"What subject?"

"The – um - subject I am about to broach." He smiled tightly. "It concerns several rumours that have surfaced regarding Damian Fitzpatrick's death."

"Sorry?"

"Rumours. About how exactly Damian Fitzpatrick died and what he was doing at the time."

I think it's fair to say I gaped. I gaped at him like a halfwit.

"Damian? Minister Damian Fitzpatrick? But…he died of a heart attack," Everyone knew this. Damian Fitzpatrick, politician and statesman, keeled over at his desk because of a heart attack.

"Heart attack." I repeated helpfully. "He died of a heart attack."

Damian Fitzpatrick died of natural causes. I wrote the press release myself.

"There are…. complications with that version of events," Doyle said. I stared at him. "You are surprised?"

"Surprised? Are you serious?" Are you insane? Is what I meant.

"Look, there was a whatsit, an autopsy thingie, wasn't there? I mean the medical examiner said he died of a heart attack. Liam Fitzpatrick, his own brother, told me. How could there suddenly now be some doubt about that? It's ridiculous."

He shrugged. "Perhaps. Nevertheless, rumours have surfaced that it wasn't natural, and that other – other circumstances led to his death."

This was mad stuff. I stood up, feeling strangely shaky. I disliked Damian, but the idea that someone could slander him in death was horrible.

You like to think there's some level people won't stoop to; I supposed some idiot had spread a rumour that he was in bed with one of his women or died snorting cocaine or something.

After all, rumours about a drug addicted Minister had circulated for years. Unless by "not natural" the man was suggesting murder. Which was ridiculous of course.

"Why are you here?" I demanded. "Why tell me all this?"

"You're about to start working for Derek Fields. You're about to start working for Michael T O'Mahony."

He surprised me by striding towards the door and throwing it open rather dramatically.

"You should be careful, Miss Jordan. Keep your eyes and ears open. And contact me if you hear anything of interest."

12

Chapter Twelve

"What?"

He was gone, the door shut behind him. Without reflection I legged it to the door and put on the safety lock and chain. I had the uncomfortable feeling that I had just had a conversation with a very unstable man, because that was the maddest tale I had ever heard.

Him and his "rumours!" And what had any of it to do with Derek Fields or even more laughably, Michael T O'Mahony?

I sat down and stared miserably at my food. Damian had died of natural causes; I was sure of it.

On impulse I grabbed my phone and searched for Liam Fitzpatrick in contacts. He answered on the third ring, his friendly still-countrified voice sounding reassuringly normal.

"Liam?"

"Caroline? Ah Caroline, how are you? You know what, I was just saying to Maureen, I wonder how Caroline is getting on! I thought I'd give you a ring next week, get you out for lunch?"

"That would be lovely Liam. In fact, I have some ideas I'd like to run past you, if you're interested. Some thoughts about projects for you, to be honest."

"Really?" he sounded pleased. "Sure, that's great. I've been at a bit of a loss, to tell you the truth. You'd miss that auld rip, wouldn't you?"

God almighty. Damian had treated him like dirt and Liam was still loyal to him, underneath it all. I sighed and decided to lie politely. I like Liam.

"You would, you really would." Decent pause to allow for feelings of the bereaved, then "Actually – god I hardly know how to raise this but – do you mind me asking you something Liam?"

"Not at all,"

"Well, it's about Damian actually, about his – well, how he died. I wondered, were they sure – I mean absolutely sure – it was a heart attack?"

There was a puzzled silence then he replied, "But of course – did I not show you the report? They said he had a massive coronary. Our dad died of a heart attack, you know. My GP tells me all the time that it runs in families. I was shocked, but you know, I don't think I was really all that surprised poor Damian went the same way. He used to get red in the face when he'd lose his temper. I often warned him, I did. "Damian," I used to say, "You'll give yourself a heart attack!" No, there was no doubt about it."

I remembered Damian's face, mottled red when he was in a rage; and there was no doubt he indulged in the finer things in life without ever worrying about his health – cigars, whiskies, good food.

My heart slowed down, and the weird sick feeling Doyle had left me with started to fade.

"Why on earth do you ask, Caroline?" Liam sounded curious but not, thank heavens, affronted.

"Ah something really stupid someone said, Liam. I thought they'd got hold of the wrong end of the stick alright. But you know what it's like, some people are so insistent they make you nearly doubt yourself."

"And they said Damian hadn't died of a heart attack?"

"Well, not in so many words, more they said they had heard a rumour about how he had died. God people are stupid, Liam, I'm sorry I brought it up at all, don't worry about it."

"Ah no, I'm glad you told me. If you can put whoever said it straight, I'd be grateful. I would hate Margaret or the boys to hear people gossiping about stuff like that."

"Oh, I know, that's why I had to ask. I don't really know what he was getting at, or even if he really knows to be honest, but it was such a bizarre thing to say I had to ring."

Liam sighed "I suppose it's inevitable. We may be grateful the gossip columns haven't tried to say he died in bed with Elaine Dunne."

"Hah! Or worse…" The words "Lillian Roche" hung unspoken in the air.

"Don't, don't. Could you imagine it?" He chuckled. "Seriously though, Caroline, I'd be grateful if we could keep this between us. As I say Margaret would be devastated if she heard rumours like that, so would the boys."

"I won't mention it to anyone, Liam," I meant it sincerely. "I only mentioned it to you to give you the heads up. As far as I'm concerned, it's pure nonsense, I wouldn't give it oxygen."

"And you'll try to find out who is spreading it? You could ask Paula?" Liam knew of old that whenever we needed to get to the bottom of a rumour, Paula was our one-woman CIA and KGB combined.

"First thing tomorrow and when I find them, I'll squash them."

"Well, I'm glad you got in touch anyway."

"Me too, Liam. The other reason I rang was, I have a bit of news. I got a job offer. I start tomorrow in fact."

"What? I thought you were back at the helm of Jordan PR!" I could hear in his voice how delighted he was to be included in the gossip.

I had found it hard going from the centre of power to a regular job – I couldn't imagine what it must be like for Liam, retreating into forced retirement.

"I am, still, technically but an old political contact got in touch. You'll never guess who?"

"Caroline Jordan, if you tell me you're working for Lillian Roche…."

"Urgh no….and much higher than that."

"Higher than a Minister? That's – oh, oh, oh! That's not it, is it? Michael T O'Mahony? Go on, it's not!"

"It is! I'll be doing a lot of media stuff for him," Slightly fudging but it never hurt to be circumspect. "I'm starting tomorrow, can you believe it?"

"That's fabulous. You'll be right in the thick of things. Oh, that's amazing," Liam sounded genuinely pleased. "Wait until I tell Maureen!" Maureen, his wife of thirty odd years was a dote, Mammy to everyone she me and genuinely interested in people. Liam was devoted to her, there would be no Elaines or Lilians popping up at his funeral.

"Well, I'll be flat out the next few weeks, probably until Christmas with the emergency budget and so on but if you don't mind, I'll be picking your brains from time to time? I'll really miss having you to run things past. Who's going to give me a heads up on all the backroom deals and stuff?"

I could hear the smile in his voice when he answered.

"Ah, ring me anytime. I may not be in the middle of things anymore but there's nothing historical I can't tell you. I know where a lot of skeletons are buried. I'm glad there's someone who doesn't think I'm an auld dinosaur!"

"Excellent. And I'm going to let you go now, except for one last thing. Have you ever thought about writing a book?"

I could sense him sitting upright at that, and I smiled.

13

Chapter Thirteen

DS Alan Doyle

"You know what?"

Claire MacPherson walked up to the whiteboard and started scrubbing furiously. From the set of her shoulders, I could tell she was pissed off about something.

She turned and faced the squad room. "See all that slurry about Caroline Jordan being Minister Fitzgerald's fancy bit? See how I've rubbed it all out?" She drew breath and pointed at David Locke. "I don't know where you get your info, Locke but you need better sources."

"She wasn't bonking him?" Locke shrugged. "Sorry, I was told that as a sure thing."

"A sure thing," she made a disgusted face.

"I've just spoken with half the department in there and they are all sure of one thing. The Minister had many women, but Caroline Jordan wasn't one of them. The worst they could accuse her of was being a hard-nosed, ambitious woman who is good at her job. And considering it's been almost a week now and there isn't any sign of her gossiping our news around the fecking place, she isn't a flighty twit either."

I knew MacPherson hated the stereotyping we had to do as part of job. Sometimes with all the best intentions, you had to play the odds, make assumptions. The idea to use Jordan to get things moving hadn't sat well with her from the beginning.

Locke looked a bit sheepish. "Sorry, and all that. But I only passed on the info I was given."

I wished he had double checked it before I had gone over to her apartment and insulted her.

MacPherson has an uncanny knack of reading minds at time. "C'mere, Doyle. Tell me you went in nice and politely, not like a jackbooted twat?"

"You've a way with words, "Graves rumbled, his head still buried in paperwork.

"Doyle?"

"I did what we agreed." I returned. "I needled her a bit, yeah but only to try to get her off balance."

"For the love of…" She stomped back to her desk. "Fecking *twats.*"

Graves let a few minutes pass before broaching the subject again. "Well then, where does this leave us?"

Claire sighed and kicked her desk in irritation.

"Like I said, I've had a discreet chat with a lot of people All career civil servants, all well clued in. I've asked every one of them if they've heard anything odd in connection to Fitzgerald's death. Without insulting any of them, I might add. Bet you by tomorrow there'll be enough rumours flying to thoroughly unsettle our man."

"Or woman," I added. "Don't snarl at me, MacPherson. I'm not Looney the woman-hater. I'm just saying, it's possible." But I like MacPherson and her criticism stung.

So, I probably should have followed up that disastrous interview with Caroline Jordan by apologizing or at least trying to smooth over the whole mess.

But I didn't.

Partly because I really had no desire to have my eyeballs plucked from my head on the end of those talons she calls nails, and partly because we all agreed having scared her at home, bullied her, accused her of being a money-grabbing slut and then telling her that her boss was murdered, it might be time to leave the poor girl alone.

Besides, it wasn't as if we weren't busy. The gentle shaking of the rumour tree yielded quite a few surprises; the first being that Elaine Dunne turned up asking to speak to Graves.

It had been Graves' misfortune to have to interview the luscious Elaine, when Minister Fitzpatrick's death first occurred. She literally wept all over him and made it painfully obvious that she was more than just a good friend to the late minister.

Graves has a naturally sympathetic face, which leads to women in particular trusting him with their deepest darkest secrets, so he's used to it - but the confessions of a bored celebrity housewife was a bit much even for him. He extricated himself from her with reassurances of discretion and sympathy, and we marked her off the list seeing as she had not been anywhere near the place anyway that day.

But the moment rumours surfaced that all was not as it might be, Elaine appeared in the lobby of the Garda Serious Crimes and Special Branch building weeping on the desk sergeant's shoulder and demanding hysterically to see DS Graves.

He tried to make MacPherson go down in his stead, but she just laughed at him.

"What? You think cos I'm a girl, I should interview her? Get on with yourself, Tombstone. She's all yours."

He returned an hour later, ashen faced and weary.

"What did she say?" Locke greeted him with an evil grin. "Did she confess to murdering him as he worked, in a failed lover's pact?"

"If she did, I win the pool," Darren Powers said.

"It wasn't a lover's pact," Graves said, "at least not with her. She's outraged at the mere suggestion that anyone would hate Damian enough to kill him, while supplying me with a list as long as my arm of people we should be looking at because they were jealous of him and hated him."

He shook his head. "That woman can contradict herself twice in every breath."

"Who's on the list?" I was interested, if only because malicious gossip so often turned out to be true. If Elaine had even unwittingly picked up on someone hating Damian enough to kill him, she was bound to mention them.

"According to Luscious, the chief suspect should be our esteemed leader."

A chorus of groans greeted this; we were all terrified that our immediate futures held the prospect of arresting the nation's prime minister.

"Second to him is the fragrant Caroline Jordan, whose evil nature is apparently unbounded."

He glared at me. "Don't get excited there, Doyle. She just hates Jordan because she didn't fawn all over her. A more likely prospect seems to be Mark Jacobs. She says he loathed the minister, and it was mutual. Which we knew already."

"But she also thinks Damian had some plan to scupper Mark – after their last altercation, the Minister allegedly said that he would see to it Mark lost his privileged position in the Civil Service."

Locke strolled up to the whiteboard and made a list. "O'Mahony, Jordan, Jacobs – first hint of motive there for Jacobs, we need to follow that."

"Then there is Derek Fields. Fitzpatrick was involved in some land deal with Patrick Gillespie,"

Gillespie was notorious in Garda circles as a bare step away from pure criminal scum. Once a pure street scrapper, what my dad called a Gouger, he now managed to stay just the right side of the law, barely. And if we could have proved even one of the many allegations against him of intimidation, bribery and threats he would have been in prison years ago.

"Fields confronted him at some drunken bash last August – both men were pretty out of it, according to Elaine. She was at the party to see Fitzpatrick but had to keep her distance when Fields came over. She still managed to overhear a lot."

He glanced at his notebook.

"Patrick Gillespie owns a bank of land on the proposed M6 route. All the little hippies protesting up on Tara had a point, you know – it seems the Minister for Justice and the country's nastiest capital swine developer were hand in glove even back then."

Everyone sat up straighter and paid attention. The proposed motorway threatened one of the most important Irish historical sites, the Grange of Meath. A few years earlier a similar motorway had skirted the world-renowned Hill of Tara, amid protests and court challenges.

While the developers had won that one, the fall out since then had been severe. Allegations of bribery and corruption had led to tribunals of inquiry into various underhanded practices.

The new regime had been careful to distance itself from the sins of its predecessors and O'Mahony had shown zero tolerance for any hint of collusion with developers.

Then the new M6 motorway route was plotted to run indecently close to the Grange and there had been howls of outrage ever since the plans were unveiled. The Minister of Transport had already been directly embroiled in several court cases over the issue.

Minister Fitzpatrick had been in Transport a few years previously when the plans were first approved; if it had come out that he was hand in hand with Gillespie, before he moved to Justice, he would have been ruined. He had publicly defended the road planning decision, insisted it was the only viable route.

O'Mahony would probably have strangled him with his bare hands if he'd found out.

"But it's hard to spin as a motive because it was Derek Fields threatening to expose Fitzpatrick. If only it was Fields who got killed, then the Minister would be an ideal suspect. Same goes for Gillespie – he had no motive to kill his golden goose."

"But it's a good lead…" Claire MacPherson frowned in concentration. "I can think of several ways in which it might have been a motive. What if Fitzpatrick got the wind up after Fields had a pop off him? He might have gone to Gillespie – maybe tried to back out of the deal? and maybe the lovely Patrick wouldn't risk his tame Minister hanging him out to dry."

"Atta girl, you just volunteered yourself. Get at it, everything about Gillespie and Fitzpatrick and how the hell Fields comes into it."

Claire shook her head, ruefully. "You'd think I learn, wouldn't you?"

"Okay so we put Gillespie, Fields, Fitzpatrick at the top of the heap," Locke rearranged his list on the board. "Anything else?"

"Eh…the Mark Jacobs angle, there was nothing really to it other than some vague memory of a comment she claims Damian made, but I still think we need to check it out. Alan," He turned to me. "You should cover that one. Have a chat with Jacobs and see what happens."

"What did you tell Luscious Elaine?" Powers asked.

"Nothing really, just patted her on the shoulder and said we'd look into it. She's quite nice, you know, just a bit dim."

Powers sniffed. "Interesting though, that she came armed with a list of suspects."

14

Chapter Fourteen

Paula Hughes

I knew from the moment I met Caroline Jordan that I wanted to work with her.

I know it sounds as if I have a massive schoolgirl crush on Caroline but it's not like that. It's just she's the nicest boss I have ever had and before that, she was the nicest co-worker I ever met. She rang me to go to lunch any time she was free, she included me in every outing or trip, she told me anything she heard that would affect me or my job.

And all through it she's been the best mate I've ever had. So, win-win all round, for me.

Besides, it's Stephen I have the crush on.

But Caroline changed my life, and I love her for it. All my life I had been slightly out of whack with everyone else; a swot in a school full of hooligans, a quiet shy girl in a family of glamour-puss extroverts and so on. Being bright got me through school and being hard-working landed me a job but it was a boring life.

My sister Anne worked as a secretary in a PR company and when a job opened up in the accounts department, she got on to me about it like a terrier with a bone.

"You'd be ideal for it." Anne is gorgeous and very ambitious in her own way. She plans on marrying a millionaire, but her ambitions on my behalf were for me to finish my accountancy exams and get a good steady job.

"She might even meet someone, if she had a good job." She regularly told my mother.

Anne's view of life was very simple; good-looking girls married boys with good jobs, plain girls got good jobs so some boy might marry them.

I'm not actually that plain by the way, it's just that in comparison to my three tall, rake thin, blonde siblings I am not that noticeable. I'm shorter, not fat but not thin, and I have unmanageable hair. That's my cross in life. I am perfectly ordinary.

Anyway, I went along to the job interview in order to shut her up, and to my shock I got the place.

The offices were perfect shiny, modern spaces in a very cool area. And although I was only a lowly accounts technician, I could still tell people I worked in Duggan and Fines, the famous Advertising and PR firm.

I settled in quite quickly, kept my head down and worked away, and occasionally Anne would waft down from the second floor, where she was PA to one of the head honchos, and regale us all with tales of debauchery.

Once the excitement of a new job wore off if I'm honest, life went back to boring. Turns out working in the accounts department of a glamourous PR firm is exactly like working in the accounts department of a truck hire firm.

I sat in meeting after meeting, the anonymous girl from accounts.

Then at one such snooze-fest, the girl across from me, a very tall, stunning looking woman with funky blonde hair with huge sparkling eyes, leaned across and said "Sorry, I didn't catch your name. I'm Caroline."

"I'm Paula," I said and then added defiantly, "from accounts."

"Ah right, I was wondering why I hadn't seen you around. The only time I get down to accounts is when my expenses are being queried."

"That'd be Lisa,"

"That's the one! God, she's a narky cow, isn't she? She acts like she works for the tax man and gets a commission on every penny she manages to claw back from me."

Lisa was a bit po-faced, I had to admit.

"Are you Anne's sister? I knew it. The pair of you have the same eyes."

The guy beside her tried to claim her attention back but she batted him off impatiently. Only Caroline would get away with that in a meeting.

"Can I ask you something? Anne says you were in the College of Commerce? Rathmines? Did you happen to know a bloke called Ray Fogarty?"

"Oh god, yes. Ray from Galway – everyone knew him."

"I was in UCD with him. C'mere, you're not the Paula who helped him move flats that time, and the two of you carried that huge TV he nicked from home down the canal?"

"That was me!" I said.

"Right," said she, "We're having lunch after this. I need to hear the stories." Over lunch we discussed the mad Ray, and we went through exhaustive lists of people to find that we knew at least three more.

That was it, so simple. But I never felt like an outsider with her, and never felt lonely in a crowd when she was around.

Caroline also got on great with my family. Most people found the Hughes clan a bit over-whelming, but she said it was a treat for her. She rarely talked about her family, but I knew the bare bones of it - her father died when she was young, her mother had never wanted a child, she was reared in boarding schools.

Her mother lived a life of parties, travel and occasional bouts of "nerves" which Caroline said were spells in rehab, drying out from the partying.

She also said she was largely guessing about her mother's daily life because once she turned 18 her mother handed her a cheque … "Your share, darling, of the insurance money. Whatever else your father was, he left us well provided for. You're going to do some course after your exams aren't you? Good time to move out, really."

Even though my lot drove me demented they were definitely more fun than Caro's mother.

When Caroline told me she was leaving to set up Jordan PR, I was gutted. When she offered me a job, as her apprentice PR executive, I almost cried with relief.

Not to be an accountant anymore (although actually, I do the accounts, seeing as how neither she nor Stephen can balance a cheque book between them. But I do them as an Account Executive.)

"You know you want to." Caroline poked me and grinned. "You're wasted in accounts. You love fashion and parties, and you are so good with people. And most importantly you have the mind of an expert strategist – if I ever want to invade a small country, I'll need you to draw up the plan. And then work out the logistics. And probably train the army."

And she was right, I am good at it. Caroline was able to devote herself to Damian Fitzpatrick while Stephen and I ran the day-to-day affairs of the company.

Stephen is amazing in a crisis; it's almost worth organizing one just to see him in action. And it's really weird because he actually panics about everything, he really does. But somehow, with him, it translates into pure empathy and all the really serious people seem to love having him around. He makes them feel special.

Caroline is a natural, she can smell out a situation in nanoseconds and she is the most charming person on earth when she wants, although she can also be truly scary if riled.

One of our very first events was for a large chain of department stores, opening up in Dublin. After congratulating Caroline on its success, the client turned to me and remarked, "You're brilliant at organization, I hope she appreciates you."

And when it comes to complicated social events like this big charity ball for cats (don't even ask) all the women want me because they think I'm so calm. In reality, I just have one of those stoical faces that doesn't show panic; sometimes I have to go hide in a corner and have a meltdown but as long as they think I am in control, everything works out fine.

The last four years had been the best of my life and I owe it all to her. Though she would vomit if I ever told her that. The thing with Caroline is, she doesn't like bull and she doesn't waste time on sentiment. But she is a nice person, despite her best efforts to hide it.

Stephen summed up the situation regarding Fitzpatrick. "I can't say I regret his demise much, apart from the effect it has had on the fortunes of our little firm." He really talks like that; he should have been born 100 years ago.

And when the job with O'Mahony materialized, Stephen and I were absolutely delighted. It seemed like a total reprieve for our little firm, our little family.

Stephen was a bit worried that she was over-doing it, "Don't fret about it," I told him. "It was the same when we joined Fitzpatrick's team." First came a steep learning curve and a period of frenetic activity and quite quickly, Caroline would find her feet and things would begin to pan out.

And it wasn't as if the Dáil didn't take enough holidays.

But there you are, we get on. And Jordan PR is ours. Well, technically it's Caroline's but the first year was so lean she paid us our Christmas bonus in shares and now she says we're all to blame if it fails. And we're good.

Stephen also worried about dealing with another Diva politician. He and I had crossed paths with Fitzpatrick periodically and he was uniformly obnoxious. It wasn't personal – he was utterly horrible to anyone he saw as a drone. He respected Caroline but even she got the rough side of his tongue regularly.

"Mark Jacobs was the only one he was civil to other than his own cronies," Stephen pointed out over a coffee. "And that was because Jacobs would have made sure no member of the civil service ever spoke to him again."

Mark was fantastic, utterly cynical while being devoted to the cause of Doing Things Right. He kept Damian under control in a way no one else could hope to emulate.

"O'Mahony isn't like that!" I argued. "Remember when he called to the office, how nice he was? He's a totally different class of person. Far better manners, for a start and far less egotistical."

And Michael T O'Mahony was so much more charismatic. My mother adored him; when she heard that Caroline was on his team she was delighted and the next time O'Mahony gave one of his famous off-the-cuff press conferences on the steps of the Dail she screamed like a banshee because she caught a glimpse of Caroline's hair in the background.

Anne rang me in great excitement one day to say she heard her boss shouting at his junior about "that Jordan bitch" stealing O'Mahony from under their noses. Stephen and I were beside ourselves when we realized word was out in the industry. Jordan PR was on the way up.

So, when Caroline told me someone was spreading rumours about Damian Fitzpatrick's death, I really didn't like it. Neither did Stephen. I couldn't put my finger on it exactly, but it felt like an attack.

"This isn't good," Stephen had his head in his hands at his desk. "Who would spread such a vicious story?"

"What's it this time?" it had been a few days since Caroline had asked me to figure out the source of the rumours.

"That he was screwing Elaine Dunne when her husband walked in, and he had a heart attack."

"Christ. You realize every second story is about Elaine? How come so many people know about her, all of a sudden?"

"She was never that discreet." Stephen rolled his eyes. "Poor cow. She isn't bright. I bet she cried on a lot of shoulders when Damian died – word gets around. Here, you don't think there's anything in it, do you? I mean the fact her name keeps cropping up?"

I shook my head. "No, I don't think there's anything in any of it. Look, first it's just a handful of people and all they hear is that Damian's death wasn't a heart attack, or somehow wasn't kosher. That's all. The details all get filled in later."

Stephen threw me a chocolate digestive "You're a wonder. You really know how people work."

To my annoyance, I could feel my cheeks redden. If only I could flirt without turning into a walking tomato. "Thanks," I said gruffly.

If I could wave a magic wand I'd come up with some witty reply or some subtle signal to make him sit up and take notice. Or get him drunk and see if he fancied me any better while pissed. Except of course we had been drunk in each other's company many a time and he hadn't so much as held my hand.

"You okay?" Stephen's face creased in concern. He had lovely eyes and a finely boned, intelligent face. I loved that he was taller than me, and that he dressed well without being fussy. And he had amazing hands, with long, pianist's fingers.

"Fine." Reluctantly I turned back to a spreadsheet detailing the outlay on decorations for Lady Foxrock's Cat ball. A load of candelabra center pieces had gone astray. And several chairs. I wondered, how could anyone lose chairs?

"Paula?"

"Yeah?"

"So, what if the original rumour was true," Stephen said thoughtfully. "I mean, all the original rumours said that Damian didn't die of a heart attack."

"Actually, they all said there was something hinky about his death. Some said he didn't have a heart attack or that he had a heart attack, but it was someone's fault…"

"Right. So, what if they're right? I mean it's a pretty weird rumour to just get started all by itself, isn't it?"

I shrugged it off. Really, Irish people would gossip about anything; if you thought there was any truth in most rumours you heard, you would end up believing anything.

But we kept digging and over the next few days I realized something odd. I called a council of war with Stephen.

"There's something wrong." I pointed at my pad of scribbled notes, where arrows pointed and looped and led inexorably to one central fact.

"Whoever spread these rumours, they all have one common source when you get right back to it. Every single one." I pointed to the centre note. Every single arrow led back there.

Whoever it was, they wore the uniform of An Garda Siochána.

15

Chapter Fifteen

Caroline Jordan

"DS Doyle is on his way down," the Garda behind the desk said. She spotted my hat, scarf and umbrella and grinned at me. "Is it still vile out?"

"It's worse," I replied gloomily. It had started raining three days before and pretty much hadn't changed, except the rain got icier and the wind stronger. I had toyed with the idea of ringing DS Doyle, but Paula persuaded me to wait until she had done more some digging around. But every single rumour led back to a high-ranking Garda source.

I was here to rip his head off.

He did not look particularly pleased to see me either, a fact I first attributed to his dislike of me on general principles. But then I saw that he was not alone. The man stomping behind him, obviously agitated, was none other than Damian Fitzpatrick's youngest son, Rory.

Rory was the unmarried, rugby loving hulk. His normally pleasant face was red-faced and angry, and to my delight, he seemed to be chewing DS Doyle's ear off. I stood to one side, unnoticed by them both, until the Garda at reception called out, "DS Doyle! Lady waiting to see you."

Rory glanced at me and then did a double take, his face filled with suspicion. I smiled warmly at him, on the very sound assumption that we both on the same side.

"Rory," I extended both hands. He took them and tried to smile graciously but a muscle still twitched in his jaw.

"Caroline?" it was definitely a question. I nodded at Doyle. "What a coincidence. Both of us here to see the same member of the Gardaí?" A flicker of something I hoped was comprehension crossed his face.

"Well, I'm on my way out. I'll talk to you soon, Caroline." He glowered at Doyle. "I'll be hearing from you very soon as well, Detective Sergeant." With that parting shot, he disappeared back out into the wild night.

Doyle gave what sounded like an exasperated sigh, and turned his fish eyed stare on me.

"Well. Miss Jordan. And what can I do for you?"

"Oh, I dunno," I spoke loudly and deliberately so that everyone in the rather busy city centre station foyer could hear.

"Let's see, a little matter of malicious gossip mongering to start. I was wondering, seeing as you're a Garda, you might be able to answer this for me. What kind of lowlife scumbag spreads cowardly, anonymous rumours around the place, upsetting a grieving family and leaving them fending off questions from friends and colleagues? In your professional opinion?"

He went red, or rather two bright red spots appeared on both cheeks. "We can talk in here..." he muttered, placing his hand firmly on my shoulder and all but frog marching me into a small room – an interrogation room, part of my brain noted excitedly. I have always been a sucker for cop shows.

He closed the door and turned to me with a glint in his eyes. "For god's sake! I suppose you think that's funny or something? Did I not tell you that particular piece of information was private?"

"Private?" I pulled out one of the chairs and sat down firmly. DS Doyle was given to towering over people and using his considerable height and muscularity to intimidate them. He had done it in my kitchen, but he was not going to get away with it twice.

I had learned from dealing with men over the years that you can never win a confrontation with a bolshy man by being bolshier. You won by taking away their power, ignoring their posturing and imposing your own power on the room.

I made myself comfortable, while he visibly fumed; only when I had my handbag, coat and scarf arranged to my satisfaction, did I glance back up and him and continue.

"You arrived at my door one evening, behaved in a bizarre and rude fashion, made an obscure reference to rumours surrounding the death of my former employer, made comments about my current employment, and then left. Oh, no, wait, you gave me a dire warning, also highly obscure, and then you left. Frankly, I took nothing you said seriously."

His cheeks went bright red in two spots again and Doyle opened his mouth to speak, but I held up my hand dismissively.

"Please do not interrupt me. Since that evening, I have heard from several sources that there are rumours flying around. Damian was with someone else when he died, Damian didn't die of a heart attack, it was drugs, it was sex, even rumours that it wasn't a natural death. I'm just waiting to hear that he was bumped off by an assassin."

"Now, DS Doyle, the strange thing is no one seems to have heard these rumours before you brought them to my attention. See, one thing I'm good at is tracking down gossip and rumours. I've had every, last, malicious little story checked and double-checked, and you know what keeps popping up? Not so much "a little bird told me" as "A high ranking Garda source told me.""

"Now that makes me very, very suspicious. I think about a high-ranking Garda official turning up on my doorstep and making strange allegations and I think to myself, could this be linked?"

I leaned back and tapped the table lightly. "Now, I don't much care what you say about Damian Fitzpatrick. He was an auld rip, and proud of it. But I do care about his brother Liam, and his widow Margaret, and his kids. I care that someone is spreading dirt that has to get back to them eventually. If I'm right about why Rory Fitzpatrick was here tonight, it possibly already has. And that's not acceptable."

He was as cool as ice; I had to hand it to him. He looked at me levelly and although his cheeks were still slightly flushed, he was otherwise unruffled.

"Miss Jordan," he began then stopped, then gave a little laugh. "OK, I'm sorry. Look, we seem to have got off to a very bad start – all my fault, I admit it."

He pulled the other chair from the far side of the table and sat opposite me. "I can appreciate in retrospect that it all must seem a bit odd. But to be perfectly blunt, I wanted to see what you would do. With the information, I mean. When you didn't do anything, I really should have got back in contact with you but - well, things are complicated."

He spread his hands in a gesture of "what could I do?"

I tapped my foot in a reciprocal gesture of "what the hell are you talking about, you unutterably idiotic man?"

"DS Doyle, I appreciate you apologizing for your rudeness – I take it you were actually apologizing for your rudeness to me? Thank you. – but unfortunately, you haven't made any of this any clearer. Why did you deliberately try to get me to spread a rumour like that? What were you trying to imply?"

He sighed. "I wanted to see if you would spread it around that Damian Fitzpatrick didn't die of natural causes."

The man was clearly insane. "But why on earth would you do that?"

"Because, Miss Jordan, I happen to know his death was anything but natural."

You what, now?

I tried to think of something to say but my mind was blank. My sparkling wit and repartee as they say, had buggered off.

A brain cell fired into action. Liam! "Excuse me, but you're wrong," I said triumphantly. "I know Liam Fitzgerald extremely well and he assured me that his brother died of a heart attack. He has a death certificate to prove that."

He looked at me pityingly. "Yes, I know. Initially that's what was assumed. The doctor called to the scene saw all the hallmarks of a heart attack and proceeded accordingly. Then when Dr O'Toole arrived, she saw something different."

Dr Lorraine O'Toole, the famous state pathologist? This sounded pretty convincing. Except, when did O'Toole examine the body? And how did they manage to keep that quiet?

"It was agreed for various reasons, most of which I can't go into with you, that the heart attack story should stand. But the truth is, he was murdered."

Something of what I felt must have shown on my face because he said, with something approaching a kindly tone of voice (rather like Darth Vader trying to be nice) "I appreciate this must be an awful shock. I am sorry we involved you but at the time we thought it would yield results. But now, you can rest assured we have it in hand. And I cannot stress this enough Miss Jordan – this is strictly confidential information. Strictly."

Flipping cheek.

"Eh, the last "confidential" information you gave me, I was supposed to actually spread around. So, which is this?" He didn't reply but had the grace to look sheepish.

I sighed. "Look, frankly, this is all a bit mad. I mean, everyone who saw poor Damian said he had a heart attack. He looked like he had one. Everyone believed it. Are you honestly telling me that if a Minister of this state is murdered, it's covered up and no one is any the wiser?"

"Yes. More or less. Look, there is more going on here than you know. For goodness sakes, think about it. The man dies at his desk, in the government buildings. Who are the suspects? Who are his colleagues, his friends? Who has motive? Do you really think we can investigate this as if it were Joe Bloggs from Kimmage?"

"I suppose not, but- but it's still mad. I still don't understand why you tried to get me involved."

I sounded a bit petulant even to my own ears, but it was hard not to feel hard done by; I had come here expecting to have a drag down fight with Doyle, fully armed with righteous indignation and now it seemed he was in the right and everything he had done was for a good reason.

This was highly annoying - as he was just the most irritating, smug, rude man and I was still not sure that he was fully compos mentis.

"Look," Doyle rubbed a hand across his face wearily. "I thought you would spread the story. I'm sorry, you work in PR, you're media savvy, you know all the people involved – it never occurred to me you'd be the only woman in Ireland to keep a secret."

He tried a smile but dropped it when I scowled. My least favourite kind of "compliment" is the one that implies a woman should be flattered by an insult to every other woman.

"Anyway," he continued hastily," I also wanted to observe your reaction. You must see, you were one of our chief suspects."

Ah here, this was going too far.

"Me? Why me?" I said indignantly. "I just worked for him - I might not have exactly liked Damian but no one did. What makes me a suspect, for Christ's sake? Hell, I was out on my ear when he died – he was my livelihood."

The look on Doyle's face was classic. Even as he opened his mouth to respond, you could see some ancient survival mechanism in the hind brain kick in, telegraphing messages like "Shut up, shut up, shut up, she doesn't know what you're talking about..."

But it was just a little too late, as the words popped out. "Well, to be honest we thought you were Damian Fitzpatrick's mistress..."

I'll hand it to him, he segued almost seamlessly into apologies as I stood up. I've been told that when I want to be, I can be highly intimidating; at that particular moment, I fairly vibrated with rage.

I deliberately opened the door wide so his colleague at her desk could hear me. Then I stalked right up to him - Doyle actually flinched as I came close.

"Say that again. Go on."

"I'm sorry, sorry-"

"You roaring idiot. What is wrong with you? Do you have a big book upstairs entitled "policing by stereotypes? I'm in PR so I must be a gossipy halfwit. I'm female working for a high-profile Minister of state, so I have to be a sodding Monica Lewinsky? What – all women are gossipy sluts who can't keep secrets? Do your female colleagues know what a low opinion you have of women, DS Doyle? Do you think they're all sleeping their way into jobs?"

"Look, I'm sorry," the man said desperately, "we knew he was sleeping with someone – look, won't you come back in..."

"He wasn't sleeping with someone, he was sleeping with two people and neither of them was me, you brain dead moron." Wrenching open the doors with hands unsteady from sheer rage, another point occurred to me.

"And even if I HAD been sleeping with him, who gave you the right to judge? That man was an unfaithful, lecherous goat but you can only blame the women he slept with! You ever consider he might have "slept his way into a job?" Oh no, cos he's a MAN! you and your misogynistic piggery"

I slammed the door shut behind me and found myself the focus of both the Garda behind the desk and the rather drunken old woman with whom she had been dealing. The Garda was grinning like a loon, and I swear she gave me a surreptitious "thumbs up". The old lush twinkled up at me and started chanting "lover's tiff, lover's tiff."

"Lover's tiff, my bum." I replied rudely. I looked at the Garda and said "You'd need to watch that one, Garda. Apparently, his view of women originates from somewhere around the Middle Ages."

"Ah he's not that bad," she said but added, "though he probably deserved that."

Too right he deserved it.

16

Chapter Sixteen

Still seething, I stalked to the car park, which for a Garda station was in a surprisingly dark and isolated spot at the back of the station. Like, you would think they would have crime prevention in mind, rather than setting up every visitor to the station as a potential car-jacking victim.

I could hear the traffic outside on the main road but otherwise it was an eerily deserted place. Usually, I would cross a car park like that with eyes in the back of my head, fists clenched around my car keys and holding my breath ready to scream.

As it was, I was still burning with rage, and completely occupied with all the other things I wished I had said to DS Doyle and not a bit aware of what I was doing, so when a hand touched my arm, I almost burst into tears with sheer fright.

I gave a strangled kind of cry and tried to run away backwards but only succeeded in tripping over my own feet.

"Caroline?" the voice sounded vaguely familiar and it seemed to know my name. "Are you OK?"

Rory Fitzpatrick. If I had half a working brain cell, I might have guessed that he would wait outside to see me. I tried to gather some tattered dignity and stand upright again.

"Christ, I gave you a fright. I am terribly sorry." He sounded genuinely

87

contrite. When I looked at him, I was shocked by how fraught he looked and despite myself, I experienced a pang of empathy. I forced myself to smile.

"It's okay – I just wasn't expecting anyone out here. Or I suppose I expected anyone out here to be a mugger."

He smiled, and I had to admit the Fitzpatrick genes were easy on the eye. Like his brothers, Rory was tall and well built. At my height, you appreciate a tall man. Whereas I could look DS Doyle in the eyes, Rory actually towered above me by a couple of inches.

His features were regular and where his brothers tended to be a little bland if pleasant looking, his face had a touch more edge. You'd pick him out of a line up, as Paula would say.

"I'm so sorry. I should have called out first, I know. But I was just so glad to have caught you – I was about to head off." He glanced around himself ruefully. "What must I look like, standing in the rain like a stalker?"

It was still pouring rain. Now I thought of it, I was freezing and wet.

"Here, sit in the car." I beeped my pride and joy, a Jaguar XK series black coupe. It wasn't brand new – almost three years old now – but it was in mint condition, and it had been the first new car I had ever bought. And the best part was I had got it for an absolute song.

A year after I began working for Damian, I had been at a party in the house of one of Ireland's favourite socialites; a great party, until I had discovered the 16-year-old daughter of a Senator passed out in a downstairs bathroom.

The poor wee girl was in a bad way, and the rather older young man who was hanging over her didn't seem all that interested in her medical state. A few hours in A&E getting her stomach pumped ensued, then her parents arrived, heard the story and expressed undying gratitude.

When the story didn't appear in the Sunday tabloids, her father contacted me to express even more gratitude (people really do have a low opinion of PR types.) Anyway, it turned out her uncle owns the biggest jaguar dealership in the country. When her father heard I was looking for a decent set of wheels, I found myself the proud owner of a car that I couldn't have afforded at the full price in a million years.

Rory looked it over appreciatively but said nothing, just sank into the seats and groaned. "I'm soaked."

I turned on the engine and hit the heater to full. "That's better." Rory twisted in the passenger seat to look directly at me. "Caroline, can I ask you – I mean, I know it's none of my business, but would you mind if I ask you – what brought you to see DS Doyle tonight?"

This was going to be difficult to broach tactfully but then again, it really had to be said.

"Rory, I came to see Doyle because I heard something. Something I needed to talk to him about."

"You heard something about my dad?" I felt so sorry for him, he looked almost sick.

"Yes. I heard a – well, your uncle Liam and I heard some rumours so we felt we should look into them. Neither of us wanted to upset your mother or any of you but we were afraid if we didn't do something it was only a matter of time before one of you got to hear them."

"I knew it." He shook his head. "I heard the same – same *lies*. One of Dad's oldest friends, Patrick Mullins. He took me aside and said he'd heard a load of rumours around the place about Dad and how he died. He- he thought it had something to do with that trollop Elaine Dunne."

He sighed, looking so miserable I had to look out the window or hug him like a child. I had always wondered if the boys knew about their dad's peccadilloes. "But then I heard – well, it was ridiculous. But I heard people were saying that it wasn't a natural death."

His mouth tightened into a closed line.

"Ah."

"You heard the same?" Rory was startled.

"Yes. Well, yes and no." A stab of conscience smote me, smote me good. I couldn't help it; I was congenitally inclined towards the forces of law and order.

A Garda – albeit a strange and probably deranged one – had asked me to be discreet.

"I heard such a mish mash of rumour and innuendo, including that he'd been up to no good when it happened and so on…I just ignored them at first, but they didn't go away. It could just be some malicious person with some perceived grudge against your family, getting a kick out of spreading muck."

"Do you really think so?"

"I don't know. I honestly don't. I mean, the death certificate was clear as day, heart attack."

"Yes, yes it was," he said eagerly. "That's what I told Doyle. Did you know Doyle was asking around about Dad? That was the other thing Patrick Mullins told me. He said he was asking all kinds of stuff, but you know what it's like, people close ranks."

"Yeah, I heard the same." It was more or less true, and gave me a chance to say, "I thought maybe he had asked questions and that had sparked off a load of stupid rumours."

Rory shook his head. "Nah. These rumours are coming from someone with a grudge, like you said. That makes perfect sense. Poor Dad, he wasn't the most tactful of men, not when he wanted something. He made a lot of enemies in his time."

He said it almost affectionately. I suppose to the family the Minister had been a tad tactless, rather than a total monster.

"I'd say that's it." Suddenly I was very tired. It had been a hellish couple of weeks, working flat out and the night was absolutely vile, and I just wanted to be at home, in my little shoe-box flat on my own couch, watching wonderful crap TV.

"At any rate, I think between us we have given DS Doyle something to think about. Maybe he'll get his finger out now and sort all this out."

"Thanks Caroline, I really mean it. Not just for going down there and sticking up for dad but for letting me vent. Christ, I feel so much better now. I was really beginning to wonder if there was something wrong. Poor Mam – it's bad enough he died so suddenly without there being anything…well, anything hinky about it all."

"I understand. And it's my pleasure. How's Margaret doing?"

"Not too bad – good days and bad days."

"I must call into her. I really meant to, but things have just been hectic. You know I am working for O'Mahony now?"

"No!" Rory's entire face brightened as he smiled. He seemed genuinely delighted for me.

"I hadn't heard, I'm so glad. I know you have your other contracts, but I gathered from Liam you would find it a bit tough without Dad."

Whatever else he had done, Damian had reared nice kids it seemed.

"Can I drop you anywhere Rory?"

"Ah no, you're fine. I'm parked down the road. Not that I wouldn't mind being chauffeured around in this." He ran a hand over the gleaming dashboard. "It's a beauty!"

I loved when people praised my baby. "Yes, yes she is. That glow of well-being you're feeling right now is courtesy of heated leather seats. She boasts cruise control, park distance control, and climate control. Also, Xenon lights, air conditioning, alarm, remote locking, climate control, radio/CD multi-changer, ABS, multi-function steering wheel...."

He burst out laughing. "You really do love this car, don't you? I don't blame you." He grinned "maybe you could take me out for that drive some day?"

Without actually thinking about it or at least not consciously, I nodded. "Sure. It'll have to be at Christmas though, the way my professional life is going."

"That's a deal. But let's not wait until Christmas. I tell you what, I'll give you a shout during the week and the first free night you have – free being any time before half nine – we'll meet up."

He clambered out before I could say yay or nay and pulled his overcoat tight against the wind and rain. "Thanks again Caroline, I'll see you soon. Hope this old Jalopy gets you home safe without like, breaking down or something."

"Cheek." I swung the Jag round and let the headlights sweep across him. "Rain sensor & headlight washers."

He was still laughing as I pulled out of the car park.

It killed me that I couldn't just tell Paula and Stephen what Doyle had said, but really, I could not justify it. And then, I realized, if I said nothing more to anyone there was a chance it might cease to be any of my business.

Not terribly rational but all the same – between being told Damian had been murdered (how freaky was that? Murdered!) and then being told the instrument of policing and civil order in this country thought I had been banging the dear, departed Minister, I was pretty much done with the whole thing.

If I was going to be absolutely honest, I was a little frightened now. While I only really half believed Doyle and while it was obvious that he could get the wrong end of the stick without the slightest effort, still – murder was a deeply ugly word and the fact that Doyle thought it was anything to do with the people I worked with pretty much sickened me.

If only Damian had had the common courtesy to keel over at home. Then it finally hit me properly; if this was murder, then things like who saw him last and what time we all left at were actually important. And that presented me with a little bit of a dilemma.

Because, like I may have mentioned earlier, I had not been entirely truthful on that point.

17

Chapter Seventeen

DS Doyle

Of course, shortly after Rory Fitzpatrick paid us a visit, we knew we were about to get a direct line on the Taoiseach himself. "Once he starts calling in favours to get to the bottom of all this, we can move a lot more openly." Looney regarded the team sternly over the top of his glasses. It made him look like a very cranky schoolteacher.

"So, I want you all ready, everything in place. Where are we now?"

I cleared my throat. I have never enjoyed presenting a report; the general back and forth of the informal brainstorming suits me better, although Claire and Locke swear I'm the most taciturn officer they know. I just don't waste breath if I have nothing to say – which makes me fairly unique around here and so I tell them.

"Mark Jacobs…. well, there's nothing even hinted about the man that could be any kind of a motive. Whatever Damian Fitzpatrick meant by threatening to ruin his career, there's no trace of it to be found now. I've spoken to people who worked with him back in Social Welfare, in the nineties, and not one word of criticism either personally or professionally. He also worked under two other Ministers for Justice, both of whom rave about him."

Looney nodded and made a note on his book. "Fine. Talk directly to Elaine Dunne and try to get some sense out the woman. Either it's a load of baloney or she remembers something specific – find out."

Graves risked a leer and a grin at me. "I'll get you her number," he said.

Powers stepped up next. "We – Locke and I – have been working the family. There's a straightforward set up there. The sons were close to the father, the marriage seems to have been stable despite his affairs. One thing we came across and we think it might be worth further investigation…. Rory Fitzpatrick and his father have been in business together on and off over the last four years."

"Rory dabbled in property development, mainly on a small scale. He was involved in building some houses in Meath, and an apartment block development in the city centre but seems to have got out just before the crash. The company he created, Grand Designs Ltd, lists Damian as a shareholder – and a director. Not too unusual, father helping son out. What is a bit unusual is that about 18 months ago they had some kind of a falling out."

A murmur of interest rewarded this news.

"Damian withdrew from everything to do with Grand Designs Ltd, and the general feeling among the few people in the know about it was that Rory had been less than honest with the Inland revenue."

Looney nodded again and made yet another note on his infernal black pad.

"Graves?"

"Actually, you want to hear MacPherson next." Graves said firmly.

MacPherson rolled her eyes at me, but discreetly. Looney seemed incapable of acknowledging Claire's presence on the team unless absolutely forced to; it was a source of legend in the office.

Like, the Gardaí can be as sexist as any other institution, but it has improved in recent years. Looney wasn't normal in his absolute disregard for women officers. It was embarrassing – especially when the officer was as good as MacPherson. She took it well, but it wasn't right.

"Sir," Claire nodded crisply. "Well, as you all know I came across Frank Gillespie several years ago, working in Serious Crimes. He was noted in a case involving intimidation and violence against a man who wouldn't sell a building Gillespie wanted. It came to nothing, of course. We have never been able to get anyone to either testify against him or even make a case against him using paper trail or finances."

She looked around the room and smiled.

"However, we do have a lot of information on him and his activities, even if we can't actually prove it. We know for example that he acquired land along the route of the new M6 motorway approximately three months before the final route was announced. I don't know how up to date any of you are on the whole Grange issue, but the basic outline is simple."

"There were at least three viable routes that would have kept the motorway far away from the site, not have caused light or noise pollution, and at the same time preserve the vast majority of the archaeology. One of these routes was favourite to be picked. Instead, another more direct, less sensitive route was decided on, in a rushed decision that made everyone unhappy – everyone except those who land was suddenly worth a small fortune."

I drew in a sharp breath. Something was making a connection in my head, but I filed it away for future reference.

"So, according to information received from Mrs. Dunne, the departed Minister was involved in tipping off Gillespie. As we all know at the time of the route decision, the head of the National Road Association was outgoing, Fitzpatrick was moving to Justice and the new Minister barely up to speed at the time of the route debacle."

So far so good – Minister Fitzpatrick tips off a developer and they both make a killing.

"Fitzpatrick's share is filtered through his son's firm, or so Revenue suspect. But then, Fitzpatrick is in Justice. Gillespie is still involved in more than just development – he's a suspect in any number of drug related and gangland related incidents."

She grinned "And it seems our friends down the corridor have long suspected that our lack of success in nailing Gillespie has not been entirely unaided by someone in the know."

She sat back and let that last bit sink in; Locke, bless him, was the first to bite.

"Are you saying that Damian Fitzpatrick was feeding Gillespie information about the investigations into his firm?"

He whistled slowly between his teeth. "That's – wow. That's some cesspit of corruption."

Looney looked at Claire in alarm. "Detective, I devoutly hope you have some basis for this?"

Claire looked at him pityingly. "Sir, I can bring DI Phillips up here if you like?"

Phillips was in charge of the Gillespie investigation.

"But he will confirm what I've told you. Damian Fitzpatrick is officially in the frame for tipping off Gillespie on a number of things from Garda activity to the motorway route. And Fitzpatrick's best mate, the one who tipped off Rory Fitzpatrick to the rumours about his dad's death? Patrick Mullins."

Looney sat forward and stared hard at MacPherson. "Mullins? Isn't he on the NRA advisory board?"

The NRA or National Roads Association, who in their infinite wisdom had decided to put a motorway through the richest archaeology in Europe.

Claire allowed herself a little smile of triumph. "Yes, Sir. That'd be Patrick Mullins all right."

18

Chapter Eighteen

Caroline Jordan

Rory picked me up at nine, around the corner from Leinster House. I was still in my work uniform of suit and silk blouse, clutching a laptop bag. He didn't seem to mind.

"I'd say you were keeping late hours, if I wasn't used to it from Dad's time," His eyes crinkled rather nicely when he smiled. I prided myself on being able to judge people by their smiles, whether they were fake or genuine. His were all warmth.

Since our meeting at the Garda station, we'd exchanged quite a few calls and texts, firstly just bitching about DS Doyle and the situation but then about work, music, friends. I won't lie when he asked me out to dinner I was delighted.

Oh, I'd a lofty resolution not to get involved with anyone while working like a dog for O'Mahony but Rory got under the radar. Also, I'd had a blooming good week, finally, and felt like celebrating.

Doyle's visit, his ridiculous cloak and dagger antics seemed like a bizarre dream in the face of the sheer terror of starting my new job. There is nothing worse than the first day in any job, especially one at which you want to succeed.

On the one hand, I was returning to a place I knew intimately, but on the other I was returning there in such a different capacity, it was surreal.

97

* * *

For those unfamiliar with it, Leinster House is an impressive, mid-eighteenth-century Ducal Palace (with modern extensions.) To say it is imposing is an understatement, and it's a living symbol of Irish history. Built by the Earls of Kildare, then the seat of the Dukes of Leinster it is inextricably linked to our colonial past, but it was also a place frequented by Lord Edward Fitzgerald, the great Irish patriot and rebel. The oldest part was used as a model for the United States famous White House, and it used to have a great big statue of Queen Victoria outside which we removed for obvious reasons. We unloaded it to the Australians.

It sits beside the National Museum of Archaeology and the National Library, across from the lovely Merrion Square park. The Seanad sits in what was once the Duke's ballroom, while a new extension houses the lackeys, flunkeys and minions of the various ministers and all their offices.

The Taoiseach operates out of another, pretty spectacular building nearby called Kildare House or Government buildings, although like most of the population I barely knew the difference until I started work there!

"You'll be working in Chaz Mahal!" Stephen roared laughing, "Built by Charlie Haughey and funded by us poor taxpayers!"

"It was a much-needed restoration," I corrected him. "And it won awards, once the philistines had stopped crying over it."

"It cost an arm and a leg, though," he insisted, "I bet the loos have gold plated taps!"

The bathrooms may not have been as posh as Stephen imagined but one thing was true at least. The offices occupied by An Taoiseach were more opulent than the ones Damian had enjoyed in Justice, with an air of brisk efficiency that was a lot more convincing than among our old team.

Inside, the hallowed office itself put Damian's style of expensive vulgarity in perspective. Walls paneled with oak from the ancient forests of Coolattin, Co Wicklow, adorned by the portrait of Michael Collins, the great Irish rebel, over a Bossi fireplace. The painting was by an Irish artist called Sarah Cecilia Harrison. Only the desk, also made of Irish oak, was similar to Fitzpatrick's.

O'Mahony was as charming as he had been in the humble surroundings of my office, but the interview was brief and businesslike. It was clear that I was apprenticed to Fields, and he would dictate access to the Taoiseach. "Do take a seat in the foyer, Caroline, Derek will along soon."

I presented myself as instructed and before I had even taken a seat, Derek Fields appeared, smiling and genial.

As he had promised, without much further ado I spent the day shadowing him; to the intense and obvious curiosity of everyone we met. Derek remained absolutely tight-lipped about my presence at his shoulder, and I took my lead from him.

Rory had listened to pretty much live commentary on my daily progress. Unlike most men I'd met, he seemed interested, and his cheerleader support made me look forward to every call.

Meeting up in person began to look unlikely though. Every day following was a whirlwind of faces, meetings, huddled talks, laborious discussions about wordings of press releases, and no holds barred commentary from Derek on Minister Roche and her unsuitability for the role of Justice Minister.

Nothing convinced me more completely that he had accepted me into the role of his apprentice than his gleeful dissection of her, the situation, our last meeting, our next meeting, everything, the moment we were alone. And nothing confirmed my hero worship of him more than his obvious distaste for Lillian Roche.

Every now and then Michael T himself crossed our paths. He greeted me warmly and then seemed to promptly forget my very existence. Up close the relationship between him and Derek was extraordinary. For four years, I'd worked with a Minister and his brother, but the rapport between the Taoiseach and the Kingmaker was a hundred times more fraternal than theirs had ever been.

"Rory, I swear to god, they have a bro-mance. Like, you'd swear they'd served in a war together and were the last survivors of their regiment or something."

Or at least so I imagined; being an only child myself I had to guess. My mother, whom I saw about twice a year at most, was not fond of children and often boasted that she had agreed to have one to keep my father happy. As you might gather from that, I am no authority on the subject of happy families.

But they seemed not only to like one another and be as used to each other as an old married couple, they seemed to share a single fundamental view of life, politics, and everyone around them. As the days wore their way through, a tortuous plan to present Roche as the ideal replacement for Justice took shape, and with every day, I realized that if Derek Fields had not wanted me there, Michael T wouldn't have even considered it.

In fact, it was clear that hiring me had been Fields' idea in the first place.

The Sunday afternoon saw an impromptu meeting in the lounge of a well-known hostelry, infamous for its political gatherings. There was Fields, two senior civil servants with important titles, a couple of party flunkies and a political analyst whose fees were rumoured to be in the tens of thousands per month.

I was the only woman, I noted sourly, Irish politics really was an old boys club at the top level, even now. The men present didn't quite snub me, but they did make it obvious that I was unimportant to them. The conversation was loaded with in-jokes and the kind of shorthand developed by people who work in the same industry. I spoke the language as well as anyone, but no one was listening, not in this group.

The subject of Dearest Lilian was raised by the TD from South Galway, an angry man who tended to loom over others and raise his voice in direct ratio to any opposition. The gathering was inclined to rebellion on the issue, but Fields firmly cut across any grumbling with the words "This is unproductive, Gentleman. The matter is decided. All that remains is to firm up arrangements." A polite way of saying we don't care about your opinion, lads.

Not five minutes later, in the process of giving detailed instructions on the next day's vote and the timing of the announcement, Michael T paused in mid-sentence, and stared at me.

"Honest opinion, what do you think the reaction will be?"

I swear to God, you could sense the sudden tension in the air. Every man there lent forward and practically sniffed the air for blood.

"Lillian Roche is loathed." Might as well jump right in. "No matter where you put her, the collective sigh of relief from every parent in Ireland, people whose life mission it is to get her out of Education, will speed her on her way. I reckon beneath the obvious sniping and grumbling, on the whole it will be a popular decision – somehow her public image suits justice."

Yeah, jack-booted and draconian. In the current political climate, the public would not mind seeing someone vicious in charge of Crime and Punishment. "Dragon Lady Calls for Public Executions…" the internal editor sniggered.

"The opposition will attack the decision, and Minister Roche will give one of her snide put-downs and then, all anyone will be able to think about for a week is whatever sobriquet she applied to the leader of the opposition."

I drew a breath and added, "Politically, as in what she'll actually do to Justice, I wouldn't dare predict. She will probably try to bully her way through it like she did in Education. But I suspect she may meet her match in Mark Jacobs. I bet you, she won't find him easy to browbeat."

A horribly long moment of silence followed, making me wondered if this would be the briefest gig of my career.

"Hah!" Michael T gave a bark of laughter. "You have Lillian pegged anyway. Mark Jacobs, eh. You may be right." He reached over and squeezed my arm. "I knew you'd have it sussed."

I caught the glances around the table between politico and lackey and suddenly the man beside me moved his chair to allow me more space, closer to the table. And everyone smiled at me.

And just like that I was "in." Or at least not so far out. After that meeting, there was a subtle change in the way I was treated, the deference that was gently proffered. The Taoiseach had made a public gesture in front of his cronies and colleagues, and it hadn't been wasted on them.

"Capitalize on it," Paula cautioned me. We had almost daily update phone-calls, the three of us. Stephen and Paula were working like Trojans to keep Jordan PR's normal clients happy, and I was so in debt to them at this point no amount of Christmas bonuses would cover it.

"I'm trying to, I assure you. Every night before I crawl into bed, I read every newspaper, devour every set of minutes, swot like I'm taking the Leaving. All so that the next time I'm asked an opinion I can be as incisive and impressive again."

"I'm glad to hear it," Stephen patted my hand. "Don't get distracted though. No parties or dates or weekend city breaks, eh?"

The irony of the situation did not pass me by, incidentally. I had taken this prestigious, high-profile job in part to preserve my lovely glamourous party lifestyle and now I was too busy and too tired to go out.

I glanced guiltily at Rory, his profile briefly illuminated by a wash of light, and he turned and smiled at me as if he had felt me look. Honestly, I know it sounds sickening, but it was a Mills and Boon moment. I'm no romantic but the look he gave me, sort of hungry and tender at the same time.

I deserve this, I told myself.

19

Chapter Nineteen

Thankfully, dinner was in one of Dublin's restaurants known for comfort and service as well as good food. There are a few that treat you like commodities on a conveyor belt (I had a deeply held grudge against one immensely popular venue whose Maître D' started telling us at six pm, as we walked through the door, "you only have the table until nine!" Every course we ordered arrived with the same admonition, we all got indigestion bolting our food.)

Rory was as attentive a listener in person as on the phone. He asked me questions like he really wanted the answer, and I found myself talking about things I usually avoided. Like family, ambitions, friends…usually I kept my small talk to politics and house prices.

"No really," his face was adorably earnest, "you can't mean it. Boarding schools shut over Christmas, you must have gone home."

He was a product of Dublin private schools too, although his parents had kept their kids under the roof.

"Yeah, but – and I swear, you can check this out – there are actual services you can hire that will take your kids and mind them over the holidays. Even Christmas. They give it a fancy name, like one year I was at an "Art Development and Portfolio" course in Roscommon. Another year she sent me to a "Confidence Building Workshop" in the UK. I was ten, that time."

He had such a look of comical dismay I had to reassure him. "Don't look so tragic! It was a laugh a lot of the time. I'm still friends with a lot of the kids I met on them. You'd see the same faces over and over, and during the Summer months especially."

This is why I rarely talk about my family; people think it was practically abusive. Whereas I know I was lucky – I was fed, clothed and housed. I was educated. It wasn't ideal but it was grand.

"Anyway, you're the one we should be worried about. How are you bearing up? Really."

"Ah." He ran his hand through his hair, making little spiky horns on either side. "Not too bad. It's…well, it's easier for the others. I'm not saying that they didn't care or weren't cut up about it, but they have families. They have kids, I guess that's what I mean."

He fiddled with a fork. "If you have kids, I think you have to go on. You have to focus on them. All I have is work, and a lot of that was tied up with dad…" He trailed off looking so lost, I caught his hand without thinking.

"It is different, definitely. You had a different relationship with him."

"Yes, exactly. We were…well, he was my dad. But we were adults together too."

I wondered what it would be like to have that kind of relationship with a parent. If my father had lived, would I have been as close to him?

"What?" Rory poked my hand gently. "You are thinking of something. Or someone?"

"My dad. I don't really remember him much, just a sort of warm, cuddly nice presence."

He nodded sadly. "I'm well aware I was lucky to have Dad, to be a grown up around him."

"Yeah but, it's almost worse. I don't know what I missed; you really do."

"There's no better or worse, Caroline. Both are crap. Losing people you love, is crap. All you can do is enjoy them, while you have them. Do you mind me asking, what happened to your dad?"

I shrugged. "He died in an accident. Car accident. He was a doctor, got called out late one night, on the way home he was side swiped by a lorry. He died at the scene." No matter how I phrase it, I knew it sounded glib, but I have no vocabulary for this. How do you say, the only parent who was interested in having a kid died and the parent I was left with wouldn't give me more than the barest information about my own father?

But Rory just nodded. "Tough. Very tough."

"So," I said, "Apart from family tragedy and the angst of adulthood, how are things going?"

He gave a delighted laugh. "Pretty good, otherwise." And we both grinned and went back to slagging off people we knew on the political scene.

By the time we were finished eating, the waiters were staring at us pointedly and removing chairs around us. The bill paid, waiters duly tipped, we strolled out into a crisp winter night.

Usually, a date going this well would have turned into drinks and a spur of the moment decision to leave the car in town. Followed by a taxi back to mine, and hopefully, wild passionate sex. That was all I really wanted from a date; long term entanglements were too difficult when you're working all hours.

I was expecting him to suggest something along those lines. However, he walked me to his car and asked for directions to my apartment. "I know you're a Cinderella these days,"

He grinned, his eyes twinkling, "Let's call it a night, and pick this up again next time. How do you feel about Sunday brunch? Ridiculously pretentious, so passe, or a civilized and charming institution?

"Hmmmm."

Okay so it was a little disappointing but on the other hand, this must be how normal people date.

"I would have to come down on the side of charming institution, as long as it's in a decent restaurant, and eggs Benedict feature."

"How daringly retro of you! I like it. Leave it with me, I'll find us the perfect place."

"So…" I smiled my best smile at him ("PR woman does outrageous flirting") "This is my block; I suppose a nightcap is out of the question?"

He laughed, a very sexy knowing laugh.

"Oh, you are a dangerous woman, Jordan. But I know your type. You'd lure me up, then have your wicked way with me."

"Would that be so bad?" I was stung.

In response he leaned in towards me, his lips brushing mine in the most tantalizing way, staring directly into my eyes, still smiling.

"No," he said softly. "But it would be too easy for you to write me off as a one-night stand. I don't want to be a one- night stand. I have plans for you, Caroline. They go way beyond a one-night stand."

Well, okay then.

20

Chapter Twenty

The best thing about my new position, apart from the obvious kudos and status, was watching Lillian Roche's face change every time we crossed paths. The first time was an absolute gift from the gods. Michael T, and Derek were closeted in his office, and of course in my capacity as Shadow, I too perched in the inner sanctum of government itself. Suddenly and without warning, Minister Roche entered for a tête-à-tête, full of the quivering self-importance that had descended once O'Mahony told her she was getting Justice.

She glanced around the room and when her eyes lit on me, sitting cozily at Derek's right hand, sifting through files that she just knew in her water contained information on her, she went red, white and slightly green in rapid succession.

She paused, her entire demeanour demanding an explanation but O'Mahony simply gave a weary wave of his hand and Derek acted as if I had always been there. She huffed and puffed but like a good wee Minister in the end she had to sit down and shut up.

After that meeting, one she conducted through gritted teeth, casting outraged looks in my direction, she plastered a smile on her gob at the sight of me, but she had yet to manage a single, civil, good morning. I of course, being a consummate professional, contented myself with grinning evilly at her over Derek's shoulder whenever I could. It was clear she would never like me, but she seemed to have realized that she was stuck with me.

I was proud of my work over the next couple of weeks.

Every contact in the political press was courted, every favour pulled, to get advance knowledge of what the press was about to say about the new appointee. I spun gold out of straw for the bitch. I obsessed over every detail and caught more than one potentially damaging mistake before it occurred. In fact, I worked for her like she was my one chick and me an auld hen. I earned myself a pat on the back from O'Mahony and a nod from Derek.

"Good girl. Personal opinion has no place in this. It's a hard lesson for a lot of people to learn but you seem to grasp it."

I had the woman barred from Twitter, a move that was greeted with relief by her team. Lilian had a habit of being indiscreet and occasionally libelous on that infernal platform. It made her very popular with a certain type of follower but only so they could re-tweet and mock her.

It took a curt instruction directly from the Prime Minister to achieve it but in the end her personal account was deleted. I think she hated me most of all for this, but it rehabilitated her public image faster than any other method.

And in all this the strange knowledge that Damian's death had not been natural almost faded from my mind. Almost but not quite.

During the delicate process of making Lilian Roche palatable to an unsuspecting public, I had to deal regularly with her hench-woman, Catherine Walsh. Catherine and I politely and sincerely loathed each other. She was very good at her job, though. I could see why Roche relied on her so heavily.

Catherine had a blunt manner at the best of times, so when she cornered me one day to ask what I knew about the "ridiculous rumours" I shouldn't have been surprised. What did surprise me was her manner.

"Why?" she said insistently. "Why are people asking about the night he died?" Worried, that's what she sounded. "It's ridiculous."

"Yeah. Well, you know what people are like, Catherine, they gossip."

"I told the cops that night, the Taoiseach had us here until late. Why is everyone acting like it's such a big deal…he died of a heart attack."

"Hmm." I murmured, sick of lying about it to everyone. It couldn't be good for my already tarnished soul.

"Well, if you were all together, even if there was anything to the rumours you are covered."

She flushed. "No. I mean, yes mainly but… there was a brief time when I was alone."

"Oh. But what of it? Look, they're just rumours." I am going to hell. "You've no motive to harm him anyway."

"Not me!" She snapped. Obviously, she regretted it a minute later, saying "I mean, no one there had any motif."

Yeah right.

"Anyway," there was a malicious tinge to her next statement, "the Taoiseach and Derek Fields were around too, and they both were alone after the meeting broke up. I heard them talking on the stairwell and they went in different directions."

Great, now both my new bosses were in the frame for murdering my old one. No wonder Doyle had thought I'd be the ideal mole. And the cloak and dagger antics didn't seem so odd now, I could appreciate the difficulty in accusing the leader of the country of bumping off his rival.

"Well, it's a good job they're just rumours then isn't it," I said pleasantly. She looked ready to spit.

Later I met up with Liam, who had taken the idea of writing a book like a man grasping a lifeline in raging seas. "I'm not a great writer," he said, "But I can tell a good anecdote. I thought I'd start there, putting together the various stories and high jinks over the years."

We had agreed that it shouldn't be a book about Damian per se, but a book by a seasoned political operative, whose brother had been one of Ireland's most famous politicians. It would have stories about Damian, obviously, but it would also draw on a wealth of knowledge about the personalities, crises, scandals and historical events of a career spanning nearly 30 years. From an idle thought, it had grown into a viable project and one the seemed to have reinvigorated Liam.

"I thought I would do a rough outline and run it past you, see if I'm going in the right direction?" he asked.

"From what you've told me, you are but I'd be delighted to read an outline.

And once you've got the back broken on it, we can arrange to read and re-read and streamline it."

I already had an agent or two sniffing around (having planted the rumour that Liam had a red-hot story to tell) and one of them, Nuala Collins, would have been my first choice anyway. She assumed Liam was paying me to promote his new enterprise, which seemed to add some weight to it in her opinion. I wondered if she thought that O'Mahony was secretly in on the undertaking. If so, I must try to get him photographed with Liam at some literary event. The man was owed for all the times he talked Fitzpatrick out of some horrendous error of judgment.

We had a happy chat about the proposed book and Liam tried out some of his anecdotes on me. It turned out he had a sharp dry wit and a phenomenal memory for details. There was no one and nothing in his career he couldn't recall in perfect detail – he would be any fact checker's wet dream.

It was also surprising how few of the best stories involved Damian; Liam had kept his ears cocked and eyes open and the things he knew about politics in Ireland would keep the public highly entertained for years to come.

"Well, I have to head home now." He grinned, "Maureen will be jealous, me out with a gorgeous young wan."

"She knows it's me. She'll just be relieved I'm keeping you out of her way for a change!"

"True, true. Oh – Caro, do you mind me asking? Have you heard anything more about those awful rumours?

"Oh that? No, no I didn't. I haven't seen that person since, to be honest. But then again, I haven't heard anything about it from anyone, so he must have been just talking through his hole."

He looked thoughtful. "Do you think? I'm not so sure. I've heard something similar."

"Did you hear the latest rumours," Liam added, frowning. "They're vicious, Caro."

I felt rotten but what could I say? I felt even worse when Rory brought it up over Brunch.

"I'm sorry," I said wearily. "It must be awful for you."

"You don't know anything about it then?"

Was it my imagination or was there an odd look in his eyes? I felt my stomach turn over. The last thing I needed was Rory thinking I had stabbed him in the back or something. "Sort of liking him" had turned into liking him a lot, and I was really looking forward to finding out what plans he had for me.

"I know what you know, there are rumours. I know that Liam is sure there is no truth to them. And I know that it's rotten for you."

Brunch turned into a long walk on the beach at Sandymount, talking about everything from childhood to whale watching in New Zealand. Rory had done the standard "backpack around the world" trip between college and work. I had done a non-standard trip around the world, working for a variety of strange people in odd jobs. Comparing notes was fun.

Again, he dropped me home, this time with a long lingering kiss that hinted at more to come.

I was quite enjoying this protracted courtship, and I'm not normally a fan of deferred gratification.

21

Chapter Twenty-One

DS Doyle

"Mark Jacobs worked in Environment." I threw it out for consideration.

Graves tipped his chair back and closed his eyes. "When?"

"Almost ten years ago." Looney said thoughtfully. "Still…"

"Well, when I checked his background, everyone I spoke to not only knew him, but they also liked him. I got the definite impression he was still in touch with most of his old colleagues. Jacobs is a high-level civil servant; he knows how to make and keep friends in every department."

Graves nodded. "So, we have Minister Fitzpatrick feeding Gillespie information while he's in Justice and no one suspects, except of course Phillips and his team. But he once meddled in the Transport folder, tipping him off for a land deal and – what? Jacobs gets wind of it, through the Dept. of the Environment?"

Transport and Environment worked hand in hand on a lot of issues – it would be a logical route.

"Again, our problem is, it's a motive for Fitzpatrick to kill Jacobs but not for Jacobs to kill the Minister. Unless Claire's idea about Gillespie getting the wind up is the answer."

Looney waved his hands dismissively. "Go on, back to it. At least we're somewhat further along."

Graves waited until we were back in our own office before saying anything further. "Claire, good work on Gillespie, it's looking like a promising enough angle."

He nodded at me. "Doyle, you continue on Mark Jacobs. It's imperative we find out what exactly Elaine Dunne overheard." He paused. "God damn it, if only the victim had been Jacobs or Fields. The problem is the wrong victim died."

Claire looked up from the pile of paperwork that threatened to swamp her desk. "Alan, what to you make of the Jacobs connection to Gillespie?"

"I don't know. It's too much of a coincidence that Damian Fitzpatrick had it in for him around the same time as Derek Fields threatens Fitzpatrick over the land deal."

"Yeah." She tapped her teeth with a biro and sighed. "OK. Say we both work on the assumption that the one with a motive is Gillespie and you shout if you turn up anything else."

Powers and Locke stood at the whiteboard; Locke rearranged his list once more. "So now we have a connection to Jacobs, and the Environment ministry." Locke was cheerful. "I like it. We're filling in the blanks."

"We're going after Rory Fitzpatrick," Powers added. "I want to find out exactly what went on with his company and the Minister."

Graves nodded. "Keep at it. We're running out of time now. Rory Fitzpatrick is about to poke a wasps' nest up there and once the Taoiseach gets involved, we have to make this one look pretty, and fast."

"Could be worse," Powers shot at him as he ducked out the door. "At least no one managed to make the Taoiseach a suspect."

"No," Graves grumbled. "Just his most trusted advisor."

I called to Elaine Dunne's house at half three that afternoon; for appearances sake, I rang from the end of the driveway to check she was in. When Graves had called on her, she had been eager, even anxious to talk. Now I got the distinct impression she wished me well away from her.

"I don't know," she said plaintively. She boasted one of those horribly strangled accents that evolved during the Celtic Tiger boom. Underneath you could hear the flat midlands tones that betrayed her upbringing but by dint of strangling vowels and an upward questioning inflexion at the end of every sentence, she managed to fake urban middle class.

"I don't know?…um, it's not..?"

"It's very important, Mrs. Dunne."

I noticed that she was easier to deal with if you kept that formality in place; call her "Elaine" and she became too matey. "We need to talk to you. I'm in the area and if you could just spare me a few minutes of your time…"

"Well, obviously I want to help –"

"That's great." I cut her off ruthlessly and started the engine. "I'll see you in just a few minutes."

The Dunne house was a palace; it boasted a front of rough, Wicklow slate-coloured stone mixed with smooth rendered walls, two large bay windows overlooking a long driveway and a front garden filled with rhododendron and lilac trees.

In the winter gloom the garden was a little bare but immaculate. The interior was sumptuous, the best of everything from the art on the walls to thick carpets or expensive, delicate rugs on shining wood floors. My hostess greeted me at the door and ushered me into the kitchen without much ceremony.

Elaine sipped nervously from a cup of coffee for the entirety of the interview; it looked suspiciously like a cold cup of coffee at that. I could tell from the way she constantly checked the clock on the wall of her Italian designer kitchen that she either wanted to leave by a certain time or expected another visitor, but she did not do what any normal person would have in the circumstance – explained that she had an appointment and ask me to be brief.

Nothing sparks a policeman's curiosity faster than not being upfront with him. If she had been openly impatient, I would probably have thought nothing of it but her attempts to appear completely at ease highlighted her underlying panic.

I settled into the nearest chair – I say chair, but really it was a back breaking high stool in stainless steel or chrome or some such, mounted on springs that sagged alarmingly the moment my bum made contact with it. I stuck one foot out against the edge of the central kitchen island to steady myself, hoping it didn't look too undignified.

She cast an indignant glance at my size twelves on her impeccable marble workstation. The entire kitchen was something out of a showroom or a magazine – though it looked as if no one had ever so much as boiled an egg in it. With a pang, the thought of my cramped apartment kitchen crossed my mind; I'd give a lot for a proper house with a decent kitchen. I didn't get much chance to cook, obviously, not in this job but someday I would.

"Mrs. Dunne," I consulted my notebook in a show of efficiency. "At your last meeting with DI Graves you were able to supply the DI with a list of names, people you thought might possibly be of interest in the death of Minister Damian Fitzpatrick. I would like to talk to you now, about some incidents you recounted."

The formal, polite approach was my refuge when dealing with women; it didn't make them warm to me the way they would have to Graves or Locke, but it at least prevented them from hating me on sight. Like Caroline Jordan. Whenever I strayed too far from the script, that antisocial aspect of my persona seemed to kicked in.

Elaine looked suitably impressed and scared. "Information?" she said faintly. "Oh no – I didn't - I mean, I don't have any information on Damian's death! I don't know what you mean!"

I gave her a hard stare and looked at my notes again, pointedly. "You didn't? I beg your pardon Mrs. Dunne but I need to be certain about this. Are you saying that you didn't tell DI Graves that Damian Fitzpatrick had an altercation with Derek Fields? Or that he had some kind of professional problem with Mark Jacobs?"

She didn't reply just stared at me sullenly. "Are you saying in effect that DI Graves misrepresented your comments, Mrs. Dunne?" I pressed.

"Oh, for God's sake." She tossed her shiny brown hair and pouted. "Well, when you put it like that – No, of course not. I did tell him some things that happened, that I happened to see when we – when I – "she trailed off, looking confused.

"I understand you were friends with the deceased," I said as blandly as possible.

"Exactly." She seized on the word eagerly. "Damian and I were great friends. I've known him, like, ages. He –um, he liked my company. I liked his. He often asked me to parties and things, not the stuffy political ones but the ones where he could enjoy himself. He worked hard. His wife – Margaret – she's nice and all but he couldn't be himself with her. She wouldn't go and have some fun with him, always on at him about his image and his responsibilities. He needed some fun."

She eyed me defiantly and repeated "He liked my company."

I sighed inwardly. Why did every young one who got mixed up with older married men flatter herself that it's her personality that attracted him?

"Mrs. Dunne, your relationship with Minister Fitzpatrick is not the issue here." Not strictly true but hopefully it would keep her this side of hostile.

"What I do need from you is as honest and complete an account as you can give of the following incidents – the argument between Derek Fields and Damian, and what exactly Damian said about Mark Jacobs. If there is any other information you can recall that might help us shed light on all this, I would be grateful if you could tell us."

She still looked a bit mutinous so I threw in "Damian would have wanted you to help. I'm sure he relied on you a lot when he was alive."

She flushed but there was a visible thaw.

"Well, I'm sure I want to help, I do."

Another anxious glance at the clock.

"Well. Derek Fields. That was just before Damian died. It was at Lily Dowd's party – like, the best party ever? Lily throws class parties, always the best of everything. She had that DJ – Ice K Rystal – have you heard him? He's like, the best ever? Lily got him because her brother works with U2, and they know Ice. I mean, you can't even get to see him in New York these days, and Lily had him for her house party."

"So, I really, really wanted to go to Lily's party. But Patrick – that's my husband – didn't want to go and-and I didn't want to go on my own, so Damian offered to take me."

She had the grace to blush at least. "Anyway, usually we wouldn't meet anyone Damian knows well at these things. They're more my friends than his – but halfway through the evening Derek Fields suddenly appeared. I don't know who he came with. Maybe the Lissadells."

The Lissadells were staples on the society pages; he was a solicitor, and she was a glamourous housewife and together they were repulsively rich.

"Anyway, next thing I know he makes a bee-line for Damian and I-I had to step away. Damian didn't like me to get involved in political stuff and well, he liked to be discreet. So, when I saw Derek come over, I stepped back a bit and let him talk to Damian. But after a couple of minutes Derek's voice got really like, loud and angry."

She frowned with the effort of remembering. "He said something like "You're not just a blackguard, you're a cheap blackguard. Gillespie has had you in his pocket for years, but this is low even for you!""

"Damian was raging - like, his face was red, and he was shaking? He kept saying "it's not true," but Derek was all like, "You're going to pay for this. I'll make sure it gets out.""

"Then he said something about Damian having to face the Garda for what he'd done. Damian got really angry then and then Lily noticed and sent over her husband to see what the trouble was, and Derek stalked off."

"Is that all you can remember of what was actually said?" I prompted. "Try to think, is there anything else, even a fragment, that you can recall?"

"Um…Okay, he –Derek – said that Damian was cheap. Oh, and that his little whelp would be sorry, something like that."

"Whelp?"

"Well yeah, like, Pup, you know?"

"Gotcha." I gave her my friendliest smile, which made her wince, so I stopped, and said "Anything else?"

"Um…Yes…as he walked away, he snapped something about criminals? Like, he wouldn't stay talking to criminal scum. Something like that?"

"How did Damian take all this?"

"Oh, he was raging, absolutely furious and he was really upset, ya know? Like, it was all such lies. I mean Damian was the Minister for Justice, imagine calling him a criminal? Derek Fields was mad, stark raving looney."

I wrote furiously, trying to catch up before she stopped being helpful.

"Okay…now about Mark Jacobs?"

"Oh. Well, okay, that I do remember now you mention it but – well, I feel a bit mean about it. Mark's always been really nice to me, really friendly. Not like that Jordan bitch. She always spoke at me like I was some kind of idiot. But Mark was always sweet to me." She looked genuinely sad. I could see why Graves didn't mind her so much. She was shallow and vacuous, but she wasn't toxic.

"Damian sort of liked him, I thought, until a few months ago." She continued. "I mean, Mark could be a pain in the neck to Damian, always on and on about what had to be done and how it should be done, ya know? Damian was always moaning about him, but then suddenly he sounded like he hated the sight of him. "That little gobshite." That's what he called him."

She looked at the clock and her hand shook slightly as she raised her coffee cup.

"Are you in a hurry, Mrs. Dunne?"

"No-No, not at all." She jumped guiltily. "I mean…well, yes I do have some things to do."

"This won't take much longer" I said firmly.

"Oh. Right, yeah. Well, anyway, one night when he was in good form, and we had been out and Damian had a few beers in him, I asked him why he was so annoyed with Mark all of a sudden. He went all quiet first, then he said that Mark was an interfering stuck-up little jobs-worth." She leaned forward. "He said that he was going to shaft him though! And that Mr. "Holier Than Thou" Jacobs wouldn't like it when the boot was on the other foot."

I wrote it all down, a glimmer of an idea forming, Elaine watching me anxiously all the while. She waited until I looked up and then said with a bit more firmness "I really do have things to be getting on with…"

I smiled. "Certainly, Mrs. Dunne and thanks. You've been most helpful."

"Oh. Good. Well, obviously, I'm glad to help."

She could hardly restrain herself at this point, ushering me towards the front door with considerably more haste than politeness. I noted the time was 4.30 pm; her husband's popular radio show finished at 4 pm. Presumably she was in a hurry to get his tea on.

I strolled down the drive, enjoying the views of the Wicklow mountains and the city below, the lights already twinkling in the early dusk. As I got to my car, I was startled to hear Elaine call out my name. I turned in time to see her running from the house waving. "DS Doyle!"

She caught up with me and caught her breath. It was a short enough run for a healthy young woman, but she looked red-faced, and she breathed rapidly.

"Detective…just – when Damian said that about Mark, he tried to sound confident…but he wasn't. Not at all. I could tell, he sounded like he was trying to convince himself, tell himself it would all be OK. I didn't think at the time that he actually had anything on Mark at all."

She turned around abruptly and marched off.

"Elaine!" I called out. She paused but didn't turn around. "Thanks. I mean it."

She disappeared back into her lovely huge house.

22

Chapter Twenty-Two

Paula Hughes

"There's something up." Stephen's face was a picture of worry. "She's not herself at all. Not at all."

We both knew there was something up with Caroline. Years of being through the mill together had given us all a sort of sixth sense about the others. Sure, she was mad busy up in Leinster House, but there was something else worrying her.

"We need to sit her down and get it out of her," He continued, "but it's a bit hard when we barely see her."

Things were (thankfully) busy, so busy Stephen and I communicated with Caro through voicemails, emails, texts -often crossing each other. But when we did chat on the phone, I just knew she was holding back on something. She was worried, too. Not just about work, there was something else.

"Tell you what," Stephen had his head buried in a pile of folders, so I couldn't actually see his expression, "We should go out for dinner tonight, talk it over. We -um – we could come up with a plan…." He trailed off.

I counted carefully to ten before saying "Yeah, that sound like an idea…" It was an issue that required a lot of discussion, obviously and one dinner led to a weekend drink and then to a daytime walk along Sandymount strand and then more drinks, and then one morning I woke up to find him making me breakfast. So, um, ill wind and all that.

Honestly, I was concerned about Caro, but I won't lie – I may have kind of milked it a bit to spend time with Stephen. Caroline would have approved, so I wasn't too guilty and besides, we were determined to get her talking as soon as we could. We just got a bit distracted.

The thing is with her being busy in Leinster House, and us being busy with …. well, new relationship and all that, there never seemed to be a good moment.

"There's still something worrying her," Stephen said solemnly, "More than the usual, I mean. Not work stuff." A pang of guilt hit me. We had let a few weeks slide by at this stage, she was still carrying some worry she hadn't voluntarily shared, and it worried me.

Another thing that worried me was this whole Rory situation. Like, he seemed lovely and all that but a Fitzgerald?

He had been in business with his dad, that much I knew. But like, what business exactly? Derek's little side projects were legendary and hard to quantify. I could easily imagine his son innocently teaming up with dear old Dad and finding himself importing dodgy goods or something.

Stephen agreed, neither of us had anything against Rory but I wish she'd met some nice-looking boy in Copper's nightclub or something.

Caroline was happy though. And I had to admit from what she told us, he was putting in the work. Dinners, theatre, turning up with coffee when she was working late. "How he got past Nick and his minions I don't know," Even down the phone line I could tell she was smiling. "But he did and not just coffee, macarons from Laduree!"

He also seemed to understand that she wasn't available a lot of the time, the advantage of being the scion of a politician I suppose. He was used to the life.

The charity ball for cats was coming up fast. It was a relatively stress-free event, and Lady Foxrock was easy to manage, even if she was as mad as a bag of snakes. Or cats.

What it was, was high profile. There would be a dozen mentions of Jordan PR in the glossy magazine that had the exclusive rights to the event.

And it coincided with a crucial government vote. "I have to be here,"

Caroline hissed down the phone. She'd run to the loo to make the call, out of earshot of the political groupies that surrounded O'Mahony. Our fearless leader had surprised everyone by announcing huge reforms to the tax system.

"He's promised the public. If this doesn't go through it'll be a huge set back. I'm going to be out front making sure the public know that any TD that votes against it, is voting to take bread from their kids' mouths!"

Usually, she'd make a quip about faking sincerity at this point but instead there was a grim determination. "If they mess this up, I'll ruin them Paula, so help me. It'll mean rich leeches pay a fair share for once. All those millionaires out in Killiney paying tax, can you picture it?"

She'd be waxing lyrical about this reform for months, the thought of losing it was killing her.

"Caro, I can manage this. Go reform the country, make O'Mahony look saintly. Go make Christmas a week early!"

Lots of events call themselves balls, but really are a posh disco in some nightclub rented for the evening. Lady Foxrock threw Balls, with a capital B. In the ballroom of one of Ireland's oldest and most expensive hotels, with everyone in full evening dress. Women argued for months over what designer full length to wear and jewelers around the city lived in fear for a few weeks each year as gaggles of socialites descended begging for expensive pieces to wear on the night.

Stephen's job was to manage our gaggle of assistants, smiling pretty boys and girls who wanted to earn a few bob to supplement their student loans. As long as they were reasonably bright and could take orders, they could be sure of some regular gigs with us, and it all looked good on their CV.

Our venue boasted an excellent catering staff, and I knew the head waiter well. Plus, this was our third time arranging the Ball, so it was a case of painting by numbers. There were the usual unforeseen circumstances of course – including a waiter arriving drunk, 25 chair covers in bespoke blue, and cream being delivered to a tiny hotel down in Offaly and three of the prizes for the grand raffle going missing for an hour - but we had food, plenty of wine, a fabulous guest of honour (an internationally renowned Irish movie star who seemed to owe Lady Foxrock a favour) so really all we had to do was keep everything running.

Early in the evening, Michael T O'Mahony put in a brief but well photographed appearance; it was a real triumph in a way, because it showed him willing to do a favour for Caroline.

"The irony," Stephen whispered, "Caroline's too busy to come, working for him! But he takes time out to come, as a favour for her…"

And the socialites were thrilled with themselves, even though he was gone before the dancing started.

It also meant a fair sprinkling of political figures, which balanced out the faded aristocrats and earnest literary types and ensured a few more column inches the next day. I was just beginning to relax.

And then I saw him. Rory Fitzpatrick, at the bar looking a little the worse for wear and knocking back whiskey. It wasn't hard to see why Caroline liked him – he was tall, well-built and good looking. He also, according to her, was very pleasant company and possessed a great sense of humour. I had to say, neither trait was in evidence tonight.

He looked surly; when a tall blonde woman approached him, and tried to engage him in conversation, he shook her off without compunction.

"That's his date," Stephen appeared behind me and hissed in my ear. "Can you believe it? He took another woman as a date to a Jordan PR event."

We exchanged looks. "He's half cut."

"I hope he has a killer hangover. That's double malt he's slinging back there."

One of the pretty smiling assistants claimed Stephen's attention and he moved off. I tried to keep an eye on Rory as the night wore on – there was something about his relentless drinking that intrigued me.

Then suddenly he was gone, his spot at the bar taken by an Irish model and her singer boyfriend. The evening wore on. I spent the best part of an hour being shown photographs of her cats by Lady Foxrock. She had turned up in an ancient ball gown over which she sported a heavy knitted cardigan that looked suspiciously homemade.

She had had her hair done especially, a classic up-do studded with diamante (or diamonds, perhaps) but the effect was slightly ruined by the strange felt hat she had jammed on top to keep her head warm – "these places are always terribly draughty."

I was rescued by her daughter in law, a surprisingly earthy, normal woman with a marked Cork accent.

Caroline had once told me that when her son brought home a nice run-of-the-mill Irishwoman as his fiancée, her ladyship had seemed a little agitated. Finally, she had interrupted dinner to take her future Daughter in law's hand in hers, and say anxiously, "I am so awfully sorry about the Famine. And everything else. You must hate us."

Una, her daughter in law, had patted the elderly claw and reassured her that she bore no grudges and they have been firm friends ever since.

"I'm so sorry," Una said now. "She really adores those damn cats. Thanks for all this, by the way, you've done a great job. She's having a ball. Hah! Well of course she is, literally. But I mean she's enjoying herself." She grinned fondly. "She's an auld dear."

"Una, do you mind me asking – who invited Rory Fitzpatrick. He wasn't on my list, so I just wondered…?"

"Rory? Oh, that will be Davina. Have you met my sister-in-law? No? You're so lucky. Oh," she flushed contritely and covered her mouth, "that sounds so bitchy! I don't really mean it. Well, I do a bit. She's a bit high maintenance if you follow me."

"I follow you. So, she's with Rory. Interesting."

"Oh, I don't think they're together, not as a couple. He's known her for years and she always bullies him into coming to stuff like this if she hasn't got a better date. Why he does it, I don't know. Habit, maybe."

"Ah right. I was wondering. You know Jordan PR used to work for his dad?"

Una shot me a quizzical look. "Paula, everyone knows that. Sure, Dublin has been talking about nothing much else but Damian Fitzpatrick for months."

"Really?" I hoped I sounded surprised.

"Of course. There were all those weird rumours and then, "she lowered her voice and leaned in "I shouldn't tell you this, because I overheard it but sure, you worked for the man. Rory told Davina that the Gardaí have applied for an exhumation order."

Stephen spotted Rory about ten minutes later, slumped against a pillar in a dark corner of the terrace, smoking. He came to fetch me, saying "I can't think of a way to talk to him without looking weird. You try!"

Reluctantly, I approached him; he looked very drunk but if what Una had said was true, I could hardly blame him. I signaled frantically to Stephen not to disappear off. The last thing I wanted was to be stranded out here with a drunk and tearful man I barely knew.

"Rory? Is that you." I smiled at him, trying to project friendly, not at all nosey, helpfulness. "I thought I saw you earlier. How are you?"

He blinked at me for a few moments and frowned. "You work for Caroline."

"That's right." Wow, thanks. I'm just her best friend but yeah, I *work* for her.

"Is Caroline here?" he looked around hopefully.

"No, not now. She had to leave early on. But I can tell her you were here. Do you mind me asking you something, Rory?"

He seemed to consider this, his head on one side and then nodded. "Ask away."

"Are you all right? You don't look the best. You look a bit under the weather."

He nodded. "I feel like a boiled zit." He waved his arm. "I didn't want to come. Davina made me. She's awful." He swayed a little. "I'm so, so tired."

I felt a real pang of sympathy. He looked worn out and sick.

"Would you not head off home, mate? It's late, the evening's almost over. Why not head off and get some kip?"

"I could. You're right." He looked around him in confusion. "I'd need a taxi."

"You know, I could get someone to call a taxi for you and then you could go home."

"Oh thanks – I don't know your name. I'm sorry."

"Paula."

"Thanks, Paula." He seemed genuinely grateful. It was impossible not to feel sorry for him, he looked shattered. He patted my arm. "I don't normally get so drunk. Did I make a show of myself?"

"God no. You just look a bit tired, that's all." Out of the corner of my eye I could see Stephen ringing our tame taxi firm. "We'll get you home and it'll all be fine then."

"Will it?" He shut his eyes and grimaced. "I don't think so. Home. Poor Dad. He never made it home."

The hair on the back of my neck prickled. "Your dad, Rory?"

"Poor dad. They're going to dig him up, did I tell you?" There was a wild look in his eyes. "Why would they do that?"

"I don't know," I soothed, "I don't know,"

"I'm so sorry." He said suddenly. He opened his mouth to add something but at that moment Stephen appeared. "Taxi's here, Rory. Come on now and I'll walk you out."

As they disappeared off, I shuddered. It wasn't just the cold night.

Caroline screamed down the phone when I told her. I had awoken her at the ungodly hour of 6 am on a Sunday morning and her initial reaction was towering rage. But the magic words "I saw Rory last night," got her full attention.

"Exhumed! But why?"

"All the rumours, I suppose. Someone must have decided to investigate."

There was silence, then, "I think you need to call over. Call Stephen. Ask him to swing by and pick you up.

"Um…. he's here."

23

Chapter Twenty-Three

It took her a while but finally all the blanks were filled in.

"They know he was murdered! They knew from the start he was murdered. Lorraine O'Toole examined him for god's sake. Then they let everyone think it was a heart attack and we buried him and now they're exhuming him…what the hell is going on?" Maybe if I repeated it often enough, my poor head would get some grasp of the mad situation.

Stephen clutched his head. "This is…."

"Insane." I finished for him.

Caroline cast me an imploring look.

"Talk to him," Stephen added.

"Rory? I don't know…if he wants to talk about it, I'd sooner wait and let him bring it up."

"Eh, no. Not him." She didn't respond so I ploughed on. "He was thinking of Doyle. You could ask Doyle."

"Are you mental? I will do no such thing. Ask that git anything? I would sooner chew my own arm off at the wrist."

"But you need to find out."

"No, I don't"

"Well, okay you don't need to, but it would be to your advantage. Think about it. Doyle is after putting you in a woejus position with Rory. With everyone. Imagine if O'Mahony found out you knew about Damian – a

scandal that could absolutely rock this government – and you said nothing…
"

"Ah."

"What I was thinking was, why not go and see Doyle. Insist that he guarantees your privacy. After all you never asked him to drag you into this. He was trying to use you and you didn't play ball."

"Ah feck you, Paula. You're right. I need to lean on him a little. Bugger, bugger, bugger."

I had described Rory's state to her and also Davina Gregory, Lady Foxrock's daughter. "Hmm." Caroline sniffed. "Thanks Paula, that's good to know. And thanks for being nice to poor Rory. God, it must be a nightmare."

I hesitated. I didn't like to point out that Poor Rory was there with another woman, even if it was a duty date, and while I didn't begrudge calling him a taxi and all that I couldn't shake the memory of that aggressive, truculent streak.

"Caroline, how well did Rory get on with his dad?"

"With his – No. Stop right there. No more, it's bad enough as it is without making a case against Rory."

I didn't like to tell her Stephen and I had already come up with several scenarios where Rory bumped off his dad.

"Just, mind yourself," I said. "It probably was just the drink, but he was weird last night. Just…talk to Doyle."

$$24$$

Chapter Twenty-Four

DS Doyle

I felt a bit malicious about sitting outside the Dunne house, waiting, but it struck me that in this vague fog of a murder anything new we could learn would be interesting. I pulled into the nearest driveway and turned off the engines.

The late November afternoon turned into full dark in a matter of minutes before 5 pm; the gates to the Dunne home swung open and a sleek black BMW seven series swung out, headlamps creating an arc across the road. I noted the license plate and called it in – Simon Crehan, Ireland's favourite rugby player.

It looked as if Elaine Dunne had moved on from Damian, but not from her old ways.

I shrugged. Part of me just couldn't help liking Elaine, she was one of life's innocents in a strange way. But her unfortunate husband – hard not to feel sorrier for him.

Graves greeted me with a dirty grin when I finally got back to the office. Dublin traffic is legendarily bad at the best of times but for some reason bad weather and proximity to Christmas sends it into gridlock. I had been absent over 3 hours. I slumped at my desk and rubbed my neck wearily.

"Well," he asked, "How did you find the luscious Elaine?"

"Informative," I replied shortly and tossed him my notebook. Graves glanced at it and threw it back with a derisory snort. "You've handwriting like a drunken chicken, Alan. Go on, give me the highlights."

"Ah feck." I stretched and yawned but he just grinned harder. Giving up, I recounted the entire conversation, including her last-minute addition. Graves whistled and tipped back dangerously in his chair. It was a miracle he got through every day without sprawling on the floor with a damaged back.

"That is very interesting." He tipped back and forwards again. "So, it confirms that Derek Fields and Damian had a row, and that it's about the Gillespie affair."

"And that it concerns Rory Fitzpatrick. Or at least we can assume that's the "whelp" he meant."

"And that according to Elaine, Fitzpatrick was righteously indignant about it all…"

"Yes, but he would be, I mean he is hardly going to admit everything to an airhead like Elaine Dunne."

"True. The bit about Jacobs is interesting. You think she knows what she's talking about?"

I considered for a moment. "Yes. I think she's as thick as two short planks in most ways but where Damian was concerned, she really seemed to have cared enough to notice stuff. She really believes he was bluffing about Jacobs."

"Right!" Graves clapped his hands and tipped his chair upright again. "Jacobs next. Off you go."

"He'll have to wait until tomorrow." I shook my head. "I rang and made an appointment for 8.30 am – he was perfectly willing; just said he had a busy day and early rather than later would suit him."

Graves shrugged. "Well, tomorrow then. There's been a bit of a development though. It might alter Jacob's attitude when he hears about it."

I glanced at my superior officer and groaned. Graves liked to horde nasty little surprises and land them on us, it amused him on some level. From the twinkle in his eye, I knew this was going to be a doozy.

"Rory Fitzpatrick must have shaken some trees all right. An Taoiseach was in close consultation with Looney while you were out wooing the Luscious

Elaine. It seems our esteemed leader wants Damian Fitzpatrick exhumed."

Ah God help us. I sat down heavily. "But we know what killed him. Don't tell me Looney chickened out of telling O'Mahony…" but there was no need to finish. Of course, he did.

Graves chuckled to himself. "There's supposed to be an exhumation order any moment now, rushed through courtesy of Michael T O'Mahony's political influence and dedication to the memory of his dear departed colleague."

Claire MacPherson strolled in from the tiny kitchenette carrying a steaming mug of coffee and laughing. "Here, I've just got a text from Locke. He's out with Lorraine O'Toole trying to explain to her, why we need an exhumation order for a body she's already done a full work up on."

Graves snorted. "If Locke can't persuade her to go along with it no one can. Looney will be chewing his desk right now."

"Ah he'll pass the buck up higher. You know he always covers his ass."

Claire waved her phone like a wand, granting our devout wishes for all this to just go away and be someone else's problem. "Anyway, let them exhume him. It gets us off the hook with the politicos and it might scare the life out of someone."

I sincerely hoped Lorraine O'Toole gave Finbar Locke pure hell when she caught up with him.

I was halfway home when my phone beeped. Cursing I pulled it out of my trouser pocket, where it was of course wedged. Jacobs' number flashed across the screen – a missed call.

Thank God, the Opel has Bluetooth; I flicked it on and dialed his number back. It rang out. I tapped the steering wheel, frowning. He probably was ringing to cancel tomorrow's appointment or rearrange it.

It was hardly worth worrying about – I'd catch him as early as possible tomorrow with or without an appointment. I kept going, the traffic still heavy at half seven. The rain started up again and all I wanted to do was get home. I glanced at the dashboard again and on impulse dialed Mark's number once more. If it rang out again, I would leave a voice message, I decided. It rang for a few rings and then someone hung up.

It took me another mile to decide to turn around; and I cursed myself heartily as I did it. For some reason, I didn't like the hang-up. I could cut back into town through the late-night shopping traffic and head up Baggot street onto Merrion Square, and into government buildings. A quick check to make sure Jacobs wasn't still at his desk and available for a chat and then, home. Half an hour extra on your day, tops, I lied to myself.

Nick Fallon was on duty again when I got to the security desk. He nodded and broke off his conversation with one of the young security guards. "It's DS Doyle, isn't it?" He smiled. "What can I do for you?"

"Mark Jacobs. He's in Justice…" Nick nodded. Of course, he would know someone as high up the food chain as Mark. "Any chance he's still here? I got a call from him asking me to call if I could…"

A white lie, as my mother would say.

Nick nodded again, obviously pleased to be able to give good news.

"Yes, yes, Mr. Jacobs is still here. His car is in the secure parking area, that's how I always know when he's still at his desk. He rarely leaves before 8 anyway, especially with all the changes in Justice at the moment. Lillian Roche, you know – she's taking over this week."

I smiled and thanked him.

"I'll just walk you up, sir," Nick said firmly. I suppose he thought even a detective sergeant of An Garda Siochána might be tempted to vandalize some of the State art on the walls or nick a bust of one of the Martyrs of the Rising.

"I do know the way," I tried, but he was already out from behind the desk and waddling determinedly towards the stairs. I would have appreciated his professional zeal if it wasn't slowing us both down. And he was chatty.

"Is it still bad out there?" Nick asked as he puffed upstairs. "It's the worst weather in years, isn't it? Flooding down in Cork and over in Galway…it'd make you think, now, wouldn't it? There might be something in that global warming after all."

He indicated towards Jacobs' offices. "Mind you, old people would tell you they remember weather just as bad, so it may just be cyclical."

Old people? Nick was hitting 65 at a gallop.

"Thanks," I knocked sharply on Jacobs' door and Nick started back towards the stairs. No answer from Jacobs; but the light was on, I could see it clearly through the glass door. I rapped again. Nick paused on the top stair and frowned. "Maybe he's down in the secretaries' offices? He's definitely here somewhere though."

I put my hand out to open the door and on impulse paused. I rooted in my pocket and found my gloves; pulling one of them back on my right hand I grasped the doorknob gingerly by the stem and twisted. I felt rather than heard Nick come slowly up behind me.

The door swung open, and I saw Mark Jacobs. He sat at his desk, a smaller less ornate version of Damian Fitzpatrick's, but a large mahogany desk, nonetheless. There were papers in front of him, scattered across the desk and spilling out onto the floor. The man himself stared straight ahead with lifeless glassy eyes. A bright red welt stretched across his neck, and the front of his shirt was stained a bright shiny red.

"Oh god," Nick breathed behind me. I stuck my arm out in time to stop him moving forward into the room. "Out." I ordered. We stepped back outside, and I shut the door carefully. Nick leaned against the wall, his face grey and drawn. The man looked ill.

"Are you okay?" He nodded. "Nick, I need you to sit down now, just here…"

I got him to a small hardback seat halfway down the corridor and he sank into it gratefully. Pulling out my mobile I punched in Graves' number. He answered on the second ring and cursed loudly when I said "Mark Jacob. He's been murdered. Justice Department offices."

25

Chapter Twenty-Five

Caroline Jordan

This was ridiculous. Utterly ridiculous. I sat down in the security office and waited for someone to tell me it was some kind of sick joke.

"Caroline?" DS Doyle sounded almost kindly as he hung over me. Well, at least not actively rude or aggressive which was an improvement for him. "Are you alright?"

Am I what? Alright? I gave him a look designed to wither blossoms on branches in Spring. "It's ridiculous," I said slowly and clearly. Why was the man so slow on the uptake?

"Look, Mark Jacobs is a friend of mine. It's absolutely insane to say he's dead."

Civil Servant found dead at desk, my treacherous little inner headline writer whispered – Civil Service Cuts, Civil Service Slasher I realized I was having a small localized nervous meltdown and tried to swallow down the mad words pushing their way up into my throat. Doyle handed me a glass of water and stepped away from me, probably out of sheer fear.

After a couple of minutes my heart stopped trying to claw its way out of my chest and my brain stopped trying to make obscene puns. I sipped the water and tried to make sense of everything.

"I don't understand." I felt miserable. Mark – poor Mark. He was such a lovely man. I really liked him. He was a friend. Everyone liked Mark. He was sharp and witty and well – yes, bitchy at times but in a really funny way.

He was my friend. We were going to have our annual Christmas drinks soon.

I'd been wrapping up some paperwork in my own office, two floors and several corridors away when the phone on my desk had started flashing. For a moment, I considered ignoring it, but when I glanced and saw it was the security desk I answered.

I was expecting it to be one of the guards trying to see who was working late or asking if I could move my car or something. When poor Nick Fallon came on the line, gasping for breath and sounding as if he was crying, it took several attempts to understand what he was saying. And then I couldn't believe it.

I had hot footed it across from my own offices, cursing whatever brain fart had made me choose high heeled boots that morning. By the time I reached Mark's office, I had convinced myself that it was all some kind of mare's nest; Mark must be ill, or maybe Nick was ill and hallucinating.

Without hesitating I reached out and opened the door – I heard a shout behind me, but it was too late. The door swung open and – the bile rose in the back of my throat again and I coughed convulsively. Doyle stepped forward and took the glass out of my hand, refilling it from the office jug. I took it gratefully and tried to stop my hand trembling.

"Miss Jordan – Caroline," Doyle sat down opposite me and spoke in a quiet grave tone. "I am terribly sorry you saw that. I tried to stop you, but it was too late. Nick rang you while I was waiting for the team to arrive – they're in there now."

"Did I mess it up? I mean, opening the door, without like a hanky or something."

"No. It's okay. We'll take your fingerprints anyway, and we can still dust the door." I had the feeling he was just being nice, every detective story I had ever read castigated the idiot who blundered in touching evidence. I would give a lot not to have opened that door for a variety of reasons.

"Well, I'm sorry, anyway. I didn't know. I thought Nick – well, I thought he must be wrong."

"Of course."

The door opened and a pleasant-faced woman stuck her head around it, eyebrows raised in a question. Doyle shook his head. "In a few minutes, Claire," he said. She gave me a sympathetic look and disappeared.

"Caroline, I'm going to get someone to take a statement from you – just when you last saw Mr. Jacobs, if you saw him this evening, what time Nick Fallon rang you…literally just run through the details. Then I'll get someone to bring you home. You can fill in any blanks tomorrow, OK?"

Home. Half of me wanted to be home and the other half wanted to cry at the idea of walking into a cold dark apartment. Rory was out of the city, on a family trip to Newry or Banbridge or some such place doing unpatriotic shopping. But I could hardly ask DS Doyle to send me some Garda to keep me company, so I nodded and tried to look as if I wasn't about to puke.

The woman he'd called Claire reappeared after an interval and introduced herself as Detective Claire MacPherson; she was efficient but kindly and she didn't push for details, just a broad outline of the day and evening.

"I saw Mark by chance this morning – he used to park right beside me but now I have a different assigned space. He pulled into his row as I was parking and came over to take the mick about it. "I knew I was babbling but I couldn't stop.

"People have a theory about the parking spaces, like that if you're a few rows away from the side entrance you're in favour and if you and up by the railings you're out of favour. He came over and asked if I had done something to piss off O'Mahony – the Taoiseach, I mean."

Tears started to well up to my utter mortification. I had not cried since I was about 14 years of age and here, I was, about to blubber all over a policewoman.

"Anyway," I sniffed, "He was in good form. He seemed relaxed. We always met for drinks before the Christmas recess, so we talked about that, and he said he had plans for a really nice Christmas. But he didn't say what, exactly."

I sighed. "We were in a rush, we were always in a freaking rush, we said goodbye on the top landing – the one out there and I went on up the stairs.

That's it. Then Nick rang me to say something terrible had happened to him."

"Go on home," MacPherson advised, shutting her notebook. "If I were you, I'd stay home tomorrow. You've had a terrible shock."

I stared at her blankly. It dawned on me rather horribly that I could no more stay home and ignore this than she could. I had to get to a phone, ring Derek Fields and fill him in. Now.

The Taoiseach couldn't be greeted by door-stepping reporters first thing tomorrow morning demanding to know why a senior civil servant had his throat cut in the Justice department. Not just a civil servant…Mark Jacobs.

A cold chill settled on me. Damian Fitzpatrick. Mark Jacobs. What the hell was going on around here.

I thanked MacPherson and she left. I had to go back to my offices to collect my bag and car keys, not the most pleasant of walks through darkened deserted corridors; my heart was pounding again by the time I locked the door of my own office and made my way back to the first floor.

Doyle was standing by the stairs talking earnestly to an older man – the detective who had come with him to interview us when Damian died, I realized. Except then he had seemed subordinate and almost disinterested, whereas looking at him now, that was clearly a façade. Now he was alert, authoritative and in control of a team of people who hurried back and forth around the crime scene.

Doyle looked up and nodded at me. "Miss Jordan. I was afraid you'd left on your own. Hang on there, I'll get someone to escort you home."

I almost refused but I bit my tongue – yes, I needed to ring Derek Fields but there was no way in hell I was walking out to my car on my own. "Thanks," I nodded at the older man as well. "If someone could just walk me to my car…"

Doyle frowned. "They'll do more than that. I'll get one of the patrol cars to drive with you and see you into your apartment."

I was too tired and sick to argue. Two friendly, softly spoken young Garda took me down to secure parking and one drove me to my apartment and walked me to my door. I made him wait while I opened up and checked the place – it was embarrassing to be such a wimp, but I felt as if every nerve in my body was on high alert as it was.

With profuse thanks, I saw them off and grabbed my mobile from my bag. Derek Field's number was on speed dial, thank Christ.

"Derek?" I tried not to gabble but I am sure I sounded like a demented beansidhe.

"Caroline?" he sounded highly displeased – I had probably interrupted his dinner.

"Derek, something terrible has happened." I told him as briefly and succinctly as I could, my voice breaking a little over the details. Some inner editor stopped me from telling him all the details, though. Let the Gardaí do that job.

"Mark Jacobs has been attacked, at his desk. He's dead, Derek. Nick Fallon and DS Alan Doyle found him this evening. DS Doyle had an appointment with him this evening, Mark was working late."

There was a silence at the other end of the line that spoke volumes. Finally, Derek broke it saying "Caroline, I'm so sorry. I take it you were still at work?"

"Yes. Nick let me know what had happened, and I went down to see what was going on. It's definitely true. Mark was dead. The Gardaí are all over the place right now, Derek. There's no way the media won't hear about this in the next half hour or so – probably already have heard. There's always someone who'll tip them off."

"That's okay don't worry. I'll go there now – and I'll ring Michael T. Are you still there?"

"No, they made me go home."

I felt slightly guilty that I hadn't rung him from my own offices when I went to collect my gear but how to explain that I would sooner have stabbed myself through the eye than sat at my desk making phone calls all on my own?

Derek didn't seem too critical though.

"Well, you've done extremely well. Thanks to you we can get in there now and get some control over this. I'll make sure Michael knows. Bloody hell, Mark Jacobs. What the hell is going on?" Fields rarely swore.

I closed my eyes and let the sheer exhaustion wash over me. "I don't know Derek, I really don't."

Well, you take care. Try to get some sleep and I'll see you first thing tomorrow. I'll fill you in then on what's happening. And thanks again, Caroline. I won't forget this."

I put the phone down on the counter top and started to cry.

26

Chapter Twenty-Six

Paula rang me at the crack of dawn. "You poor creature!"

I could hear Stephen in the background making comments along the lines of "Tell her we're on our way over."

I groaned and tried to roll over, but the bedclothes had bunched themselves around me like a shroud. It had been a long, and mostly sleepless night. In the small hours of the morning, I had seriously considered knocking myself out by drinking a bottle of vodka but the idea of turning up to the worst day ever in work with a stinking hangover stopped me. As it was, I felt hungover with tiredness.

"Paula," I croaked. "What time's it?"

"It's seven o'clock. We're in the car and about ten minutes away from you."

"How did you hear?"

"Derek Fields," Paula said in hushed tones. "He actually rang my mobile this morning at like, Half five. He said we were to make sure you were okay. Well obviously, the minute we heard we were coming over anyway, but – well, he was really worried about you,"

Well colour me surprised, sometimes the shallow and cruel world wasn't quite so callous after all.

I pulled myself together enough to climb into the shower and then to unlock the front door and stick the coffee on.

A glimpse of myself in the bathroom mirror was frightening; I looked old and haggard and sick. It took some serious make up to render that image vaguely human. By the, Paula and Stephen had burst into the apartment carrying Danish pastries and surrounded me with a group hug.

Usually, I'd have sacked them for anything as twee but this morning I leaned into it gratefully and let them fuss over me.

"You've to come in when you feel up to it, but as early as you can," Stephen announced. Obviously, Derek's word was law with my loyal employees.

"And – it's all over the papers, Caro. And the radio."

"No details though, "Paula added. "Just the basics. A high-ranking civil service found dead at his desk, foul play suspected, solemn statement from both the Garda Commissioner and An Taoiseach -"

"Wait! An Taoiseach?"

"Yep, Michael T himself. He made a very dignified statement "Dreadful, terrible tragedy, united in grief and sorrow for Mark's family, dedicated colleague and loyal servant of the state..." He did it really well and it pretty much was from the steps of the Dail at the crack of dawn. Vowed to hunt down the perpetrators and asked for the nation to join him in outrage at this violation of our sacred national seat of power. That sort of thing."

No wonder Derek had sent the troops in to mind me. He must be thanking his lucky stars I was around last night.

The first thing that anyone would think of now when the hot news story of the day cropped up was O'Mahony's comforting, accomplished leadership. And no one did the human touch the way he did.

As an added bonus I could go to work knowing that someone else had taken charge, at least initially. It was going to be a media frenzy all the same – and on top of that there was the not inconsiderable issue of a murderer wandering around.

I won't lie. It was a somber moment when I passed Mark's office that morning; I couldn't help looking at the door and remembering the scene of the night before. I sighed, and stomped on past, trying to ignore the curious glances from every passer-by. People were discreet enough, no one actually stopped and pointed at me, but a whisper seemed to break in waves both in front of and behind me as I walked.

Derek was waiting for me on the top corridor, his face drawn and tired but as usual he was impeccably dressed and exuded confident authority. His first words were delivered in his clear, carrying voice.

"Michael says to go into him as soon as you're settled, he's very anxious to make sure you're okay."

I could see the faces of the staff change imperceptibly – with one careful sentence I had gone from being a Jonah, a bearer of bad news, to one of Michael T's main concerns on a terrible morning. I smiled gratefully at Derek – at least now I'd be spared some of the more malicious gossip that was bound to break out.

I was full sure that various reports already had me as the victim, the murderer or an actual eyewitness already.

My warm glow was short lived; there was a pile of notes on my desk, every single one of them a message from some journalist trying to get an interview or at least a comment.

"You should see Derek's pile," one of the administration staff said. She gestured to indicate a pile three feet high.

"I swear to god the phones have been hopping. And not just from journos! Everyone from the Vintner's Association to those wild-eyed savages from Moral Majority have been trying to get a foot in the door. Everyone seems to feel they have something important to contribute to the investigation, like their opinion."

"Any psychics?" I crumpled the nearest pile of phone message sheets and threw them expertly into the wastepaper bin.

The girl – Samantha, I remembered her name in time – smiled and shook her head. "No not yet. But plenty of ghouls."

"That's the way of the world, Samantha. Sadly, when something remotely newsworthy happens people want to be in on it, no matter how inappropriate it is. Ignore everyone, answer no one, cut journalists off at the knees and tell them there'll be an official press conference soon. Just repeat that like a mantra.

Don't stray off script – if you so much as say you're busy you'll see yourself quoted in the newspapers tomorrow under a headline "Samantha from the

Taoiseach's office suffers breakdown in murder aftermath.""

She giggled but nodded. "Will do. I'll spread the word around not to engage at all."

"Thanks." Time to go face the big guns. "Anyone with the Taoiseach?"

"Oh no!" she assured me her voice tinged with awe. "Mr. Fields told us to keep everyone away until you got in, he's waiting for you now."

Obviously, she thought the great man was paralyzed without instruction from his right-hand woman. I would have enjoyed it immensely if I were not feeling as sick as a parrot. The horrible feeling that had settled in the pit of my stomach at the sight of poor Mark's body just wouldn't shift. Breakfast had only been a slice of toast but even so, I felt as if my food was sitting on a rock. There was a cold feeling around my throat and words had to be forced up through a fog. I supposed this was shock or trauma or something.

Michael T was sitting in one of the large leather armchairs that he favoured when not sitting officially at the helm of the state, behind his enormous desk. He rose as I entered and strode across holding out both hands.

"Caroline! I'm so glad to see you." It was impossible not to be charmed by the man, it really was. He was not exactly good-looking (although by the almost troll-like standards of Irish politicians, he was a beauty) but he had charisma and sincerity. Faked sincerity, a lot of the time, but in politics that really didn't matter.

"I appreciate you coming in today, I can't imagine how hard it is for you. It's a terrible, terrible, tragedy. I can hardly believe it even now, it's just … grotesque."

"That's a good word."

I sat down in the other armchair as he crossed to one of the inlaid rosewood cabinets and opened the lid to his private drinks' cabinet. For a moment, I thought he was about to offer me alcohol and to be honest I would have accepted a large vodka gratefully. Feck it being 8 am, I could spend the day gently pissed and get a taxi home.

Sadly, he just retrieved two crystal glasses and poured me a large tumbler of water.

"Thanks."

"I also need to thank you for your promptness last night, in letting us know what happened. It must have been such a shock for you, it would have been quite understandable if you had simply given way to personal feelings."

He took one of my hands and patted it.

"I knew I was right about you; I knew it when I saw how loyal you were to Damian Fitzpatrick. That's the only currency that lasts in politics, Caroline. Loyalty. It's a precious thing and should be treasured. I treasure the fact that you put this administration, me, the party, above personal trauma."

Okay recounting it now, it sounds unbearably hokey and twee, but the reality is at that moment I felt ten foot tall. Yes, I know, it's a bit sickening but instead of feeling like a shit who put work needs above grieving for a friend, I felt like a loyal and trusted ally. And right then anything that could make me feel marginally less awful was wonderful.

I begin to see why people join cults.

$$27$$

Chapter Twenty-Seven

O'Mahony settled himself in for business.

"Now, we need to decide how to proceed from here; obviously, we need to work closely with the Gardaí. I need to rely on you there. I need you to make sure that we're kept in the loop, as well as controlling what information we allow the media to get hold of."

He looked thoughtful and added, "And of course we need to be seen to do everything we possibly can to facilitate the Gardaí. I don't know how to tell you this…there may be a question of more than just the death of poor Mark."

He pursed his lips and shifted uncomfortably.

"I know this is going to just be yet another awful shock for you, but I feel it's important to let you know and that you hear it from me, rather than have some journalist blindside you with it." He dropped his voice, "It appears that poor Damian's death may not have been a heart attack."

Oh shit, yes. Damian Fitzpatrick's murder. I had actually forgotten that in the face of the brutality inflicted on Jacobs. It was of course part of the same mess, wasn't it? Damian Fitzpatrick and Mark Jacobs. And I was definitely not supposed to know about Damian.

I hoped the blank look on my face would pass for shock and surprise.

"Yes," he sighed heavily. "I know. It's just unbelievable. I never imagined that anything like this could possibly happen. A Minister of state murdered at his desk and then – that outrage last night. Animals!"

"I don't understand.... Damian died of a heart attack...didn't he?" I murmured.

God I am going straight to hell. Visions of Sr Assumpta rose again along with the headline "PR Firm implicated in mass murder investigation." My mother would never forgive me.

"I know, I know! As far as I was concerned Damian died of a heart attack. Then Rory – you must know Rory, Damian's son? He came to me and said he had heard some rumours circulated about his father's death. He was distraught, asked me to help him squash the gossip. Of course, I agreed."

"But when we – Derek mainly – made some inquiries, it became clear that someone was deliberately setting about the story that Damian's heart attack was a cover up. The problem of course is that...well, we can hardly have the country buzzing with rumours about a Minister's death being covered up by this Government."

Oh god, I realized suddenly – Rory came to him hoping he would use his influence privately to quell the rumours but once O'Mahony got a whiff of potential scandal, he went the other route and demanded that everything be dragged out into the open and hence the Exhumation order.

Which Rory still hadn't mentioned to me, despite telling Paula and Stephen about it? Maybe he was too drunk to remember.

"Well, as you can imagine it wasn't quite what Rory and the family had hoped for, but I persuaded Margaret that this was the best course of action. I never dreamed for one moment that there could be any truth in it – well, no one could have."

Michael T looked genuinely distressed.

"But it's official. Dr Lorraine O'Toole has performed the autopsy."

"Again?" I thought. "They're getting their money's worth out of the poor woman."

"And it appears Damian was killed by an injection of pure nicotine into the back of his neck. I don't follow the medical jargon myself, but I understand it's a lethal poison and death must have been instantaneous."

"Dear God," I said faintly. Those absolute barefaced liars. They had managed to avert the disaster of telling the Taoiseach they had considered him a suspect and hidden the murder of a Minister from him – not only that but he now blamed himself for dragging it all into the open.

I opened my mouth and shut it firmly again. It might be galling how neatly they had got themselves off the hook, but they had also rescued me from an invidious position at the same time.

"That's just dreadful. It's all so terrible. I suppose we're lucky they did the exhumation so discreetly…"

"Don't" he mopped his forehead with one hand. "It's bad enough that it has to come out now but at least we have some control over the situation now."

Derek Fields slipped into the room and claimed Michael T's attention. He cast me a sympathetic look but was gone again before I could ask what he thought of it all. As he departed, Michael T patted my hand.

"Caroline, I hate to ask but if you feel up to work…"

I pulled myself together and went out to face the rest of the day. And a vile one it was too. About half the morning was spent planning some kind of campaign to keep O'Mahony's administration on top of the situation, and then I was ushered into one of the downstairs offices to meet with DS Doyle and DI Graves.

Both seemed a little shocked that I was in work at all, let alone taking over a liaison role with the investigation. Most media and PR types are supposed to be ruthless, and it must have looked as if the stereotype was all too true. If I could summon the energy to care I would have been mortified.

DS Doyle was actually almost human, but it was only a slight improvement in his case. He grilled me, and every member of the staff, relentlessly. I answered so many questions by the end, I wasn't actually sure what the topic was – you answered one question only to have yet another pulled from the answer.

It was wearying, confusing and gave me a new respect for career criminals. I would sooner face a horde of thirsty journalists than a Garda investigation any day.

As it was, I just tried to plough through the day. Paula and Stephen pulled everything out back at the office and cleared the decks so they could come help. I hardly had a moment to speak to them, but it felt better knowing they were around.

Paula texted me at intervals to keep me abreast of what was going on in the building in general – Derek was delighted.

"Your own spy system," he remarked approvingly. "It's the way to go." He seemed charmed by the pair of them, and they in turn were full of hero worship. "They're quick learners Caroline, they reflect very well on your firm."

DI Graves seemed a little put out at being saddled with a full-time observer, no doubt seeing me in turn as O'Mahony's spy, but he was a realist. There was no way he was about to conduct the state's first murder investigation in the houses of the Dail without political oversight. He read and re-read the memorandum from the Taoiseach introducing me and asking him for his full co-operation in keeping the Office of An Taoiseach in the loop several times, sighing all the while.

"Count yourself lucky it's me," I told him finally. "It could have been one of the political goons, who would start asking you to fix their parking tickets. Or one of the bean-counters, asking where you get your paperclips and how much do they cost."

He gave me a grudging smile and waved me to a seat in the corner of the tiny office.

"As long as you're able for this, Miss Jordan. It can't be pleasant after your experience last night."

"Anything that helps," I snapped. DS Doyle gave me an unreadable look but said nothing.

The afternoon wore on, with interview after interview with cleaners and security staff, some of Graves' team flitting in and out with whispered messages. I tried to concentrate but frankly it all just blurred after a while. I kept my ears open for any mention of Damian or the night he died, but the entire focus was on the previous night's events – who had been in the building (three cleaners in this wing, none of them on Mark's floor, all the security staff and myself) and what their movements had been throughout the evening. The questions were painstaking and routine.

Had they seen Mr. Jacobs – a yes from one of the cleaners who had heard him moving about and had popped her head in to see if he wanted her to hoover or leave it until he left.

"He said to go on and do the other rooms first, that he wouldn't be long." "Did he say was he expecting anyone, or how long he thought he might be?" Doyle prompted. I looked at him in surprise; he himself had been expected surely?

The cleaner shook her head. "No, just that he'd be a while longer." And so on, through all the normal staff who would naturally be around at that time of night.

Next came Mark's colleagues, civil servants who were red eyed and scared looking as they crept in to be interviewed. Each of them cast a look at me in the corner; some seemed reassured by the sense of O'Mahony's presence even by proxy. One or two looked resentful, and I fancied a little unwilling as a result to talk freely in front of me. Doyle soon shook them out of that; the man lacked charm, but he was a terrier in an interview.

The first victim was Lisa Protheroe, one of the mainstays of the administration staff in Mark's department. She was a well-preserved middle-aged woman, with carefully arranged hair and an artfully made-up face; I had worked with her a lot while on Damian 's staff and had always liked her. She was one of the ones who looked relieved to see me sitting there.

Doyle asked her variations on the same questions he had asked everyone else – had Mark mentioned anything to her, any appointment that night, any problems, any misgivings or fears.

Lisa answered clearly and carefully but there was really nothing she could add. "He seemed much the same as normal," she finished helplessly. Doyle pounced on that phrase. "Much the same…then he was a little different than normal?"

Lisa looked startled. "Um, well, I don't know. I don't mean precisely that he was different." She glanced at me as if for help before adding, "Mark's been a little down recently, just in general. I think he found Minister Roche hard to deal with – she can be very abrasive. But he was used to it with Damian Fitzpatrick as well so it wouldn't have been anything he couldn't handle."

"But it got to him?"

"Well- no, not exactly. It was more – he would normally take that kind of thing in his stride, but it seemed to affect him more because he was worried about something else."

Doyle sat back looking pleased with himself. Lisa added, "I think it was something personal, I think he broke up with his partner a while back. I thought maybe he was still upset over it."

I looked up in surprise. It was news to me the Mark had been seeing anyone – he'd been resolutely single as far as he had told me. I caught Doyle's eye and raised an eyebrow. I couldn't tell from his impassive stare if he'd received the message that this was odd, or whether he thought I was just twitching.

"Why do you think it was personal?" Graves smiled at Lisa and she visibly relaxed. Graves definitely had the charm in the team.

"It was just – the one time I heard him get really rattled with Roche, the Minister I mean, was when she was pushing him over some paper that she wanted finished asap. He said he was going home at a normal hour for once, that he had things to do. So, I thought it was work interfering maybe, with his personal life."

Another colleague confirmed that he had been worried about something or other.

"Mark was usually unflappable. He used to stand there and let Damian Fitzpatrick hurl abuse at him and not turn a hair. But recently he was definitely more snappish. Personal stuff? I don't know about that. I think maybe, yes, and it didn't help that he really couldn't stand Lillian Roche."

"Was that really affecting him so much?" I couldn't help myself. I blurted out the question. Normally a Civil Servant wouldn't answer too bluntly in the presence of outsiders, but I caught him on the hop.

"It did get to him, yeah. She is nearly as bad as Fitzpatrick was for throwing tantrums, but he wouldn't take it from her. I think he just didn't respect her. And Mark really was a stickler for things being done properly. He hated any kind of mess or half measures, and Roche is – well, she isn't that concerned about how things get done, as long as they get done."

Graves interjected. "Yet you think it was something else that worried him?"

"Yes. Yes, I'd say it was more his own personal worries made it harder for him to take her nonsense. But it was only an impression, mind. His work was impeccable, absolutely impeccable."

But even those nuggets had to be dragged out of people, and they seemed so vague and nebulous I couldn't begin to see how it would help. A thumping headache started behind my left eye, and I spent several of the interviews wondering if I was having a stroke.

Finally, Graves stood and called a halt, as the time neared half five. "That's about all we can do here today," he said. "It's been productive." How? I wondered.

He looked at me and shook his head. "You should go home Miss Jordan."

I laughed bitterly. "Sorry, I have another couple of hours ahead of me yet."

I wasn't exaggerating. By the time, I had collated all the information I'd heard that day, passed it to Derek and debriefed both him and O'Mahony on the day's events, I was shattered.

I had a quick huddle with Paula and Stephen before sending them home and arranged to talk to them properly the following morning, then returned to have a few more words with Fields and O'Mahony. Normally to be called in for an end of day chat and relax would have been a source of satisfaction; reserved for a job well done and a sign that I was holding my own and building a relationship with the Taoiseach but today I was shaking with the desire to leave and get into my own lovely car and just put the entire day behind me.

At last, O'Mahony deemed himself able to leave; I almost wept with relief sitting in my car in late evening traffic.

I thought about calling Rory and stopped myself. Much as I wanted to cry on his shoulder, I couldn't fail to notice that he hadn't so much as texted me to see how I was.

So much for that, then. I suppose he had his own worries; but it was a bit depressing to think the only romantic relationship in my life was with a man who had barely laid a hand on me and could not call me in the midst of a national crisis.

Something sparked in the back of my brain at the thought of phone calls and on impulse I hit the Bluetooth and dialed Paula's number.

"Oy." I didn't wait for her to finish her greeting. "You said Derek Fields rang you at half five this morning. And that Stephen and you set out right away."

There was a pause then, "Yes…"

"So, what the hell was Stephen doing in your apartment at half five this morning?"

I could hear her blushing.

28

Chapter Twenty-Eight

"It just happened," Paula said, trying to sound nonchalant. She arrived on my doorstep about an hour after my phone call, red-faced and a bit anxious. "We've always got on..."

"You've always fancied the face off him, you mean."

"Well, yes. Okay. I fancied him. But he's never even tried it on, even on a drunken night out. I thought he wasn't interested."

"So, what changed?"

She went even pinker and avoided my eye. "Well – it's sort of your fault."

"Go on."

"We were worried about you, especially before you told us about Damian Fitzpatrick being murdered. We knew there was something up and we were trying to work out what it was...before you told us about Doyle and Fitzpatrick and everything, we kept meeting up to talk about it. Then one night Stephen said he'd a confession to make and that he was really trying to find excuses to get me out for dinner or a drink after work..." She trailed off, looking so happy and silly I had to laugh.

"That's brilliant. No, honestly, it really is. I think you're made for each other. Just don't fall out – I can't afford to lose either of you."

"We won't." Paula promised. She sounded so confident about it; I felt a pang. How lovely it must be to just know someone really cared about you, no bullshit, no games. I knew Stephen would never mess her around; and

I thought bitterly, I bet he would ring her if she discovered a body in the office some night.

"So, you really don't mind?" she asked anxiously. "We really wouldn't do anything to jeopardize work or interfere with the firm, you know that."

"I know. No, I'm delighted for ye both." I yawned. "Janey, I'm sorry. I need to crash. I got no sleep last night. I thought I wouldn't tonight either, but you've cheered me right up."

I saw her off then locked up and headed to bed. The apartment block, like most new Dublin blocks had street doors opened by a code and then interior block doors opened by the same code. My apartment was on the fourth floor of a five-story building so I felt reasonably safe; only the most determined burglar could scale the smooth frontage to my tiny and probably dangerous balcony.

If anyone had suggested that I would sleep like the dead that night, I would have laughed hollowly but in fact within a few minutes I was comatose. It was a deep, untroubled sleep right up until the moment I suddenly awoke and realized there was someone in my bedroom.

I'd always thought if someone broke in, I would know what to do; I sleep with a samurai sword by my bed and a small hammer in the bedside drawer. If anyone dared break in, I imagined, I would leap screaming from the bed, use the moves I remembered from my three-week long course in self-defense (5 years ago) and then draw the sword and chase them from the building.

In reality, I lay there with my eyes screwed shut listening to the pounding of my own heart in my eardrums. For the second time in 24 hours, I wondered seriously if I was having a stroke. Could I have imagined it? Some sound had roused me from sleep and then I had just known that I was not alone. I seized onto this as the only coherent thought in my head; surely, I must have imagined it. Something had woken me up and I had just leapt to the conclusion that there was an intruder. Trying to calm myself and breath normally I lay as still as possible and strained to hear.

There was nothing. I started to draw breath again.

Then - the unmistakable sound of a drawer being opened and closed. The roaring of blood around my body started again and I swear I felt my heart contract. There was actually someone in the room.

Surely, they could hear me, I was breathing raggedly, and my heart must be audible, it was thumping so hard. There was a slight scuffle as a shoe brushed off the edge of my dressing table; behind my eyelids I thought I could detect a shadow falling across the bed.

I wanted to scream but was in the grip of a paralysis; all I could do was lie still and wait.

Then after what seemed like eons, I heard a tiny noise by the bedroom door and the slightest squeak of the hinges as it opened carefully and was softly closed behind my uninvited visitor.

Minutes passed, as I tried to hear what was happening in the living room. It took me at least ten minutes to risk lifting my head from the pillow and then, groping around with trembling hands I felt on the bedside locker for my mobile. Luckily, my phone is attached to me at all times and recharges while I sleep.

Ring 999, that's what I should do. But what if they were still out there and heard? Mark Jacob's poor white face floated unbidden into my mind.

Text! I grabbed it and silently texted both Paula and Stephen's phones "Help. Call Gardaí. Intruder." I flicked through contacts, silently praying that I had put it in – yes! DS Alan Doyle, mobile number. I texted as quickly as my fingers would allow. "Caro Jordan. Intruder in Flat. Please help. Please."

That was all very well, I told myself but there was nothing to say any of them would be up, or even check their phones if they hear a text. You need to ring 999. I know, I answered myself crossly, but what if he's still out there. My inner self was being extraordinarily obtuse in a crisis.

There was nothing for it – I crept out of the bed, nearly weeping at every creak of the springs and tiptoed across to the bedroom door. I opened it a mere crack and put my eye to the gap.

The living room seemed to be utterly deserted, and in complete darkness except for the ambient light that came from Dublin's dockside development outside. My heart rate began to slow from Cardiac Arrest to mere witless panic. I waited a few more minutes and nothing stirred.

At last, I turned away to finally dial 999; the second I did there was a creak of floorboards in the living room, followed by a click as someone's hand opened the front door of the apartment. Trying not to howl in terror, I looked through the tiny gap just in time to see a figure silhouetted against the low lighting from the fourth-floor corridor outside. It paused in the doorway for a fraction of a second then disappeared, closing the door behind it.

No Olympic sprinter could have cleared the distance from my bedroom door to the front door in a faster time than I managed. Choking back tears, I jammed the deadbolt back on the door and then the chain. Didn't I do all that going to bed? I wasn't certain. I thought I remembered doing it as soon as Paula left.

There was no way I would have left any of the security devices undone, not tonight. So, that meant someone had just waltzed in past them, like they were nothing. The same person who just wandered into the Dail, the most secure building in Dublin, and managed to murder two people.

Or was I kidding myself? I had been exhausted. And in a sort of giddy elation in reaction to Paula's gossip. Maybe I hadn't put the deadbolt on, but I was 100% sure I had locked it. Or at least 80%.

That stroke was looking ever more likely. I backed away from the door and started to punch 999 into the mobile. The calm tones of the operator asked the nature of my emergency and I managed to choke out "Police, please."

Now you know the way in movies, you ring 999 and the operator is calm and understanding and talks you through the situation?

In my life to this point I had had occasion to ring the emergency phone number three times – once, at the scene of a car accident; once to report a small but sturdy fire in a front garden (don't ask) and now to report an intruder. And the common response on all three occasions?

Brusque and impatient dismissal.

The operator robotically insisted on phone numbers and names and addresses which, let me tell you I was eager to give them but apparently, I was talking double Dutch, or the operator was hard of hearing because it took so long, I was afraid dawn would break before they actually agreed to let me talk to the police. When I was finally put through, the tone of voice was less comforting authority and more bored disbelief. Finally, I managed to convey that I wasn't in fact ringing just to annoy them but was genuinely the victim of a crime.

"Has the intruder left?"

"Yes, yes, but please come anyway, they just walked in, they could walk in again."

I knew I sounded hysterical, but I really didn't care.

"There's a car on its way to you, Caroline. Now, just try to calm down a little."

Obviously, the emergency operator also thought I was a potential stroke victim. Calm down, me hole.

I lean against the wall and struggled to get a grip on myself; it was short-lived effort. A fist suddenly pummeled on the door, while a familiar if hard-to-place voice shouted "Caroline! Miss Jordan!"

I let a yelp out of me, and the operator said sharply "Are you OK? Who is that?"

Hah, I thought, you'll believe me now!

"Miss Jordan!" There was the unmistakable sound of a shoulder being applied to the door. "DS Doyle! Open up!"

"Oh, thank Christ! It's one of yours," I told the operator and wrenched open the door. The man who only weeks before I had viewed as a cold-eyed nuisance caller looked at that minute like every young maiden's dream.

"Doyle." I gestured helplessly at the phone and miraculously he seemed to understand, taking it from me firmly and introducing himself to the operator. "I'll stay with her – get that car here asap!"

He gestured to me to shut the door again. "The boys will ring up when they get here."

He sat down heavily on one of my kitchen bar stools. Now I had a chance to look at him he looked as if he had run across Dublin to get here. In fact, he looked as if he had jumped out of bed to do so; he had that "dressed in the dark" look.

He caught me examining him and gave a short laugh. "I was just going to bed when I got your text. I called out the troops and came running." His face darkened. "Want to tell me what happened?"

As calmly as I could I recounted the events of the last few minutes. He shook his head, disbelievingly I thought at first but when I hotly insisted that there had been an intruder he laughed again and apologized.

"No, sorry, I do believe you. What I can't believe is, I almost ran straight into the fecker. Or that you almost saw him. Or that he had the nerve to break in here. Why though?"

That was the question repeated over and over – Paula and Stephen once again came to the rescue and this time, insisted I leave and spend what remained of the night in Paula's apartment. Doyle looked on in amusement as they fussed over me.

"They're right," he offered, "Get out of here and try to get some sleep. At least have some company." He glanced around at the scene of crime officers busily fingerprinting every surface of my once pristine apartment. "I'll lock up here when we're done and drop the keys into you at your friend's."

Stephen drove us to Paula's, while we tried to make sense of the whole episode.

"There's only one solution that makes sense – someone thinks you have something or know something."

"But I don't! I know nothing, I have nothing. Things just keep happening to me, that's all. But I know absolutely nothing."

"Well – maybe you do?" Stephen turned to look at me in the back seat, his clever face alight. "Just think. You worked for Damian. You knew Mark Jacobs well. Is there any possibility you know something or have some papers or something? That you don't know are important but are?"

I shook my head. "Nice try, Mate. But there's nothing. No memoirs, no." I stopped short. Liam's book. Well, the outline of his book. And his papers – all kinds of crap, memorabilia, notes collected over a 30-year career…I kept them in the bedroom chest of drawers, mainly because I didn't want them cluttering up the tiny living room.

I'd stuffed Mark's short stories flash drive in there too, after the funeral. I began to feel the panicky heart pounding again. The last thing he ever gave me, his last writings, please let them be there!

"Oh blast!" I pulled my phone out of my handbag and hit Doyle's mobile again. "Yes? What's up?"

"In my bedroom. There should be a manuscript, in a smallish blue folder and then a box with lots and lots of papers and files in it…"

There was a pause. "Yes. We found the box, it's been emptied out – the papers are all over your kitchen floor, and…there's a small notebook, and a flash drive on a key-ring. I didn't see a manuscript – in or out of a folder."

I took a deep breath.

"Is there any chance? It's loose, just wrapped in a bit of bubble wrap…" I held my breath. I could hear muffled sounds, rustling of paper and then "No, it's gone."

"That's what they were after." I couldn't explain why I felt so certain, but I was. It was something in all that pile of paperwork. At least Mark's stuff was there.

"OK. Look, get some rest, I'll be over in the morning and then you can go through what we've found here – you might notice something missing."

I could have cried again in sheer frustration. "I doubt it. I barely had time to look at them…but Liam might! Liam Fitzpatrick, Damian's brother. They're his papers. He might remember something that's missing…"

"OK!" Doyle sounded quite upbeat at that. "We'll get him in to look through them. Hey, it's something. Don't worry."

It might be silly, but I felt a bit better.

29

Chapter Twenty-Nine

On Doyle's instructions, we none of us said anything about the break in at work the next day. When he arrived at Paula's the following morning, and realized I was about to go to work he was incredulous. "Janey Mac, you must love your job," he said.

"Actually, I do." I was too tired and worn out to bother being defensive. "And O'Mahony – that would be An Taoiseach to you – needs me there. That's the price we pay for the fame and glory, you know."

He grinned. "Much like my own job then. Place would fall apart without me." He tried to persuade me to stay home nonetheless but I refused. Frankly, the idea of being alone right now was anathema.

The day was pretty much the same as the previous; I went from briefing meetings with O'Mahony and Fields – mercifully short meetings as they were out and about for most of the day – to sitting in on interviews and discussions between the Garda investigating team and staff members.

Finally, Graves heaved a sigh and reluctantly pulled a file towards him. "Well, better get to it…"

I looked at him enquiringly. "Minister Roche. We have to interview her. She was in the offices until half 7 the night before last. It's unlikely to place her in the window we think the actual murder occurred but it's close enough to mean we have to ask. Oh, and of course we have to ask her about her predecessor."

A thought occurred to me. "You do know about…" I trailed off and glanced at the two other Gardaí present. They were engrossed in a conversation. I leaned forward and said quietly, "Lillian Roche was Damian's lover. I don't know if you knew that."

Graves whistled and shook his head. "You're not serious?"

"Yes. He was banging her and Elaine Dunne for the last couple of years. I just thought you'd better know before you tackle her."

I added for good measure, "She's a wagon and she hates me. If you get on the wrong side of her, she'll be extremely vindictive. I don't know if you can cover your back in some way on this one, but if you can, do."

I didn't sit in on that interview – I doubt Lillian would have stood for it at any rate - but it was unnecessary anyway. Graves promised a full transcript for me to give the Taoiseach and when I next saw him, he made a beeline for me, shaking his head ruefully.

"You didn't exaggerate, did you? She's some piece of work."

"How did it go?"

"Oh hopelessly," he said cheerfully. "I'll end my career directing traffic on the Aran islands. I had to question a Justice Minister about her whereabouts at the time of a murder and then ask her about her sex life. I'm doomed."

I didn't see Doyle at all the rest of the day; Liam Fitzpatrick spent hours closeted with him going through the remains of his papers. I caught Liam before he left, and we hid in one of the small offices for a chat.

"I'm so sorry, Caroline," Liam's kindly face as creased with worry. "If I'd thought for one second there was anything in those papers that could cause you bother, I would never have asked you to look through them."

"Oh, don't be daft, Liam. It wasn't your fault, not in any way. Did you find what was missing?"

"Well, there's definitely some bits and pieces missing, some financial papers mainly. I have to cross check against what I have at home, but I think it was stuff from Damian's land deals. But they were really pretty meaningless – standard straightforward stuff. I can't imagine why anyone would break in for them."

"Me neither, but there's got to be something in it. Look, will you do me a favour? Give me a shout when you figure it out and tell me what exactly was missing?"

"Of course." He paused and said a little awkwardly, "Um, the detectives did say I was to keep it to myself, not tell anyone."

"I'm O'Mahony's eyes and ears on this one. He needs to know pretty much everything they do, especially as his second-best media officer is the one who got burgled."

"Well, when you put it like that –, "Liam smiled, "Hell, we have to stick together, eh?"

* * *

Paula rang me at half six. "You're coming home with me," she announced. "And Stephen is going to cook us dinner."

I opened my mouth to object – partly from stubbornness and partly because after all Paula and Stephen had just got together and I was genuinely reluctant to get in the way. But really there was no way I was looking forward to spending the night on my own. Doyle rang my phone shortly afterwards to confirm that I was not – in his words- going to be an unmitigated idiot. I was too shattered to be affronted.

Stephen barely had the spuds on – no fancy cooking for us, steak and mash all round – when my phone rang. "Rory." I sighed. "What will I do?"

Paula and Stephen exchanged glances. "Well, he should have rung you… " Stephen volunteered. "But he has his own worries." Paula reminded us. "Feck it," I said, and answered.

"Caroline!" He sounded genuinely distraught. "Oh my god, are you alright? I only got back from the North an hour ago – I've literally been swamped. I went to visit Margaret and she went mad, asking how you were, why had no one called her to let her know…it was the first I heard of it. I can't believe it!"

"Rory," I couldn't keep the annoyance out of my voice. "It was all over the news. ALL the news, north and south. You couldn't have missed it. How? No one remarked to you that your father's ex undersecretary was murdered?"

He sounded confused. "Well, yes of course. Or course I heard about poor

Mark Jacobs. That's partly why I was so swamped; there's been all kinds of things going on you don't know about. There's not just Jacobs. Caroline, they think poor dad was murdered too."

He paused, obviously waiting for some kind of response. Oh yes. I keep forgetting I am not supposed to know about that. I murmured shocked phrases and he ploughed on. "So, I had to deal with lawyers, and phone calls home and all kinds of things, I just never had a chance to ring."

I had to ask.

"So, it didn't occur to you that I might have been upset and might have appreciated a call?"

Again, there was an air of confusion on the other end of the line.

"Well, I know you were friends with Mark, obviously! But, Caro, this is my father we're talking about here, honestly, I don't think you quite understand how awful this last week has been for me?"

"Really? Worse than discovering one of your friends, someone you've worked with for over 4 years, sitting at his desk with his throat slit?" Paula and Stephen tried to busy themselves in the kitchen and ignore the rising hysteria on my side of the phone call.

There was total silence at the other end of the line and then, "Oh my god. Caroline, I didn't know. Oh god, that must have been…I'm so terribly sorry."

He really did sound not just contrite but deeply upset. And it had, as he pointed out, been a hellish week for him too. I sighed.

"Caroline? I swear to God I had no idea. All I knew was what I heard on the radio – Jacobs was murdered. I saw you in the background at one of the press conferences, I was going to text but…well, to be absolutely honest I thought you must have heard about dad by then and I was a bit pissed off because you didn't text me."

Ah. Again, kept forgetting about Damian's murder.

"I – Oh feck it, I suppose I understand."

"You do? Ah Caroline, I'm so glad. And I'm so sorry…if I'd known I would have come back down, no matter what."

Is it ridiculously soppy that I felt better immediately he said that? It was nice to know that there would have been a strong shoulder to cry on if only he had known.

"And then when Mum said you had been broken into – Liam told her this morning and she has been going wild ever since."

Margaret Fitzpatrick had worried about me – that was possibly the most bizarre thing to have happened in the last three days.

I won't bore you with the rest of our conversation, but Rory volunteered to escort me home after work and look after me. Paula and Stephen greeted this with mixed feelings.

"I think he probably is telling the truth," Stephen pronounced after exhaustive analysis of the entire exchange, "He probably can't think about anything but his dad right now. But – well, he didn't exactly make his intentions clear before all this, did he?"

I cast my mind back over the couple of weeks of dating, pure dating, we had enjoyed. Dinner, coffee, phone chats, email but no real move from Rory.

"He's a slow burner? Or well, I suppose the man had just lost his father and then found out he was murdered. He's making the effort now."

And, I didn't bother adding, I like him. So, sue me for being an optimist.

30

Chapter Thirty

A late-night conference between Paula, Stephen and I had yielded a plan of action.

I was going to tell Rory I had heard rumours about Damian's death, as he already knew, and that I had gathered from reading between the lines at my interview with Doyle that there might have been some truth in them. I would apologies for not raising the issue sooner and talking about it with him, and then, thankfully we would all be up to speed and on the same page and I could stop trying to remember what murders I did and didn't know about.

"You'll feel much better once it's all out in the open," Paula opined. "Well, obviously not all, I wouldn't tell him how much you knew and how soon, but far more honest than things are now."

Another thing I got off my conscience that evening was poor Mark's flash drive of stories. His parents were elderly and had retired to Galway, so his siblings were taking him there for burial. I wondered if there might be something on the drive to comfort them, a poem or story. Mark's stuff was edgy enough, I wouldn't risk handing over the drive to the family without checking it over.

The last thing they needed was a story about hating his middle-class family or deep-seated sibling rivalries.

"Could you, Paula?" I couldn't face it myself. "If you could I would be so grateful."

"No worries." She pocketed it and hugged me again. "I'll make sure there's nothing that would hurt feelings on it."

"Thanks. They won't mind sexy bits" Mark had written some well received gay romances the previous year and his parents had been delighted with his success. "Just nothing that might be a bit too close to home."

There, I told him silently. Still have you back, mate.

The next day wasn't quite as unreal and horrible; knowing Rory was coming to pick me up that evening did a lot to cheer me up.

Neither An Taoiseach nor Fields were in Dublin that day, so most of the general day to day stuff went with them. Graves and his team were used to me at this point, so I hid away with them, shamelessly ear-wigging on the various conversations, interviews and leads. With Paula and Stephen on point duty I could afford to keep out of public view, at least for one damn day.

Claire MacPherson seemed to have taken a liking to me, she put my name in the pot whenever coffee was being made and occasionally asked my opinion on one of the faces around the political scene. It was oddly restful.

Doyle asked me gruffly if I was all right, the first time our paths crossed, and then went back to generally being tightly wound and uber-focused. He seemed to take the whole business as a personal affront, glowering at the computer screen or personal file as if he could choke the answers out of it.

Graves was laconic, calm, but he was scarily alert underneath a sleepy exterior. And Locke was a pure flirt, I had to slap him down on an hourly basis.

Liam rang me around lunchtime, triumphant and excited.

"I cross checked everything; Maureen helped. It took all morning but I'm fairly sure I've got it. There were two financial papers, they were actually in Damian's desk at home. Margaret gave them to me to look at and they got mixed up in my papers because they were from the period just before we moved to Justice; just papers to do with a land deal out near the M3. But Graves seemed to think it was important so maybe that's it?"

"Jaysus. So that's what it was."

"Well, yes, though there was one other thing, it was a letter Damian wrote me a couple of months ago. A memo, really. But he posted it rather than emailed it – I don't really know why."

"What was in it?"

"Well- "he hesitated. "It was just about his share of Rory's company. He wanted to get out of it, and he wanted me to approach Rory about it."

I chewed the end of my pen. "I know he had a share in Rory's land company, but I thought it was Rory who wanted to buy his dad out."

"Oh, it was…at least, I think so. To be honest, I was just glad that Damian and Rory seemed to have patched things up, so I didn't really give it that much thought. I reckoned Damian just wanted to get it sorted and not have another fight over it."

"So, he asked you to do it?"

"Exactly. Anyway, there was just one thing in that letter – I didn't think of it until just now. Damian wrote something on the lines of "With any luck it'll look as if I was never more than a sleeping partner." Which I thought was odd because firstly he really was no more than that, he couldn't have found the time to be more if you'd paid him. Then as well, what did it matter? Unless of course…"

Unless of course Fitzpatrick was yet another Minister involved in shady land deals and corruption. "Maybe he was afraid something he had done would crop up and affect Rory's business."

"That's what I was thinking. You know, Damian had his faults, and I won't say he was above some dodgy dealing in his time, but he would have done anything to protect his kids."

Liam was right; if Damian had known one of his shady deals would come back to bite Rory in his ass, he would have tried to cushion him from it. He would, of course, have withdrawn from Rory's firm, even if it meant upsetting his son.

I made a mental note of it and wondered if I might bring it up with Rory tonight.

In the meantime, it seemed only fair to share with Graves and the detectives. They all stared at me intently as I recounted the tiny nugget Liam had imparted, and then they looked at one another.

"Thanks,"

Graves nodded and the conversation went on as if I hadn't interrupted. It was hard not to feel a little hurt although I could see that it wasn't the most earth-shattering development. Then about two hours later, apropos of nothing in particular, Locke turned to me and said, "Run that past me again."

It took a minute to remember what it was he meant.

"Um, Liam said there was one other thing in that note Damian sent him. It was just a comment along the lines of "With any luck it'll look as if I was never more than a sleeping partner."

Locke and Doyle exchanged significant looks.

I shrugged and went back to working my way through the 900th email of the day from Fields.

"Miss Jordan…" Powers, bless him, seemed to be the youngest in the team and by far the politest. Everyone else had been calling me Caroline from day two. He held up a file – one the brown covered "special" files that were held on all employees of the Taoiseach.

Security files. "Derek Fields." Oh, my giddy aunt on steroids! he had Derek Fields' file.

Derek Kingmaker Field's actual special branch file. There were people who would pay a million euro to have a look at that; I would, given half a chance. I had to stop myself reaching out and snatching it from the Garda's hand.

"Yes?"

"Have you ever heard of him in connection with a developer named Patrick Gillespie?"

"Only in the sense that he loathes Gillespie. Everyone does. Well, everyone who isn't utterly corrupt."

Powers looked taken aback at my honesty. Whatever switch in my brain that normally functioned as the media filter, making me evaluate whatever I said before it popped out, had frizzled and blown out a few nights back.

It felt good.

"Look, Gillespie is extremely rich and very unscrupulous. He's also as rough as a badger's behind. He owns land, buildings, firms, and is a bad landlord – grand, so do many rich people. But Gillespie is – different. He owns people. He buys them up. You can't be around political circles without coming across him, everyone knows what he is. Derek Fields is one of the few people with the balls to tell him to his face."

I had everyone's attention now, whether because this was the frankest speech I had made in their hearing or because Gillespie held some special interest for them, I didn't know.

"Derek has often pushed O'Mahony – and other leading politicians – to recognize that Gillespie's a criminal, no better than any drug dealer. He often made the Chief whip get involved when a party member bought into one of Gillespie's deals. He was fighting the wind, you understand – nothing can keep a politician out of a land deal if that's what they want – but at least he tries. Gillespie's scum and it's a scandal how much he gets away with. But he would get away with much more if it weren't for Derek."

Powers sank back in his seat and frowned again at the computer screen. "Thanks" he added almost as an after-thought.

I shrugged (I might as well, it was the only exercise I was getting) and returned to my always increasing email burden.

Well, I was being honest with them; that was all I could do. A niggling feeling of guilt rose up. I had not been exactly completely honest with them right back at the beginning. Back when we thought Damian had died of a heart attack. It had been a tiny lie and I had only said it because Mark said it. But on impulse I went in search of Doyle.

"DS Doyle?" I found him in yet another small office sifting through paperwork. With a strange frisson, I recognized it as the papers from my apartment. "Can I talk to you for a minute?"

He looked surprised but waved me in. "I remembered something." I paused. "Well, to be honest, I remembered lying about something."

His blue eyes turned cold again, and that ever-present anger I could sense bubbling away under the surface rose again.

"Look, there's no point being annoyed. It's your own fault. You said Damian died of a heart attack. I had no reason not to believe you."

He sort of twitched at that.

"It was the morning after he died, and you were interviewing Mark Jacobs and me. You asked when we had last seen him, when we had left the building, that kind of thing."

You know, you would think I would be nervous admitting to a senior Special Branch police officer that I had lied to him but really, I was quite insulated from any strong feelings. It was all quite calm and peaceful.

And of course, there is always a nice virtuous feeling when you clear your conscience.

"Mark said he had left at 8.45, give or take a few minutes. I said I left at 6.45. Well, that's not strictly true. I heard Mark tell you what time he left at; he saw me leave at a quarter to seven and thought I would have no way of knowing what he said was true or untrue. But well, what I didn't say was, I came back."

"Back to the offices?"

"Yeah. I came back at nine thirty, to pick up a file I needed for the following morning. It was a choice of coming in early the next morning and trying to make it across town for a meeting or come back that night and collect it. I came back. And I saw Mark in with Damian at half past nine. But," I said hastily, as DS Doyle almost rose out of his seat. "I saw Mark leave him."

"He left Damian's office just as I came out of mine. He didn't see me, but I had a clear view of him in front of me, all the way down to the secure parking. Nick and the boys left the security desk unmanned – they must have been out the back on a break. Damian was alive and well and pacing his office as I passed. So, you see, it really didn't matter. Mark left Damian alive – not that we knew at the time anyone actually needed an alibi."

Doyle looked as if he was having apoplexy. "And you only decided to tell me this now?"

"Well, yeah. Look." God, I was tired. "At first I just thought Mark wanted to keep things simple. Even when you told me Damian had been murdered, I knew he had been alive when Mark had left him."

Doyle opened his mouth and shut it, paused, tried again and then seemed to give up.

"Miss Jordan. In view of what you've been through in the last few days I am not going to do what I should do – and that's arrest you for withholding information."

He rubbed his eyes as if in disbelief. It was an oddly childlike gesture. "I think you must on some level understand that lying to the police is wrong, stupid and wrong. I am going to assume that realize this and that you don't take it quite as lightly as you seem to."

I was quite indignant at this. I didn't take it lightly at all. In fact, I had broken all my own personal rules in volunteering this information.

Really, sometimes you can't do right for doing wrong. Even the purest of intentions can be cruelly misconstrued.

"Well, DS Doyle. I am sorry you feel that way. But now you know, for all it changes anything. Mark Jacobs had a meeting later than he said with Damian Fitzpatrick. And just so you know, Mark was definitely arguing with Damian – I heard their voices raised before I saw him come out of the room. I assumed Mark didn't want it spread about that he had given a Minister of State a heart attack by yelling at him."

I stood with my most dignified expression. "I hope you find the information of some use." A dignified exit, I felt.

Back in my own office – I thought it best to hide out for a while in case DS Doyle went roaring into DI Graves and dobbed me in – I realized I may have been a bit harsh on him. But he really was a difficult man. And it was quite hard to concentrate on anything in particular, so I settled down to clicking open each email and reading it before deciding not to do anything just yet.

31

Chapter Thirty-One

DS Doyle

When I told Graves the little bombshell Caroline Jordan had dropped, he just chuckled. "I bet she was as cool as cucumber too, when she told you."

"She actually had the nerve to chastise me, for not being grateful." I replied.

He shook his head and laughed. "That young woman is having a small nervous breakdown. And no wonder. That O'Mahony is one cold fish pulling her into work after the other night."

"She's a fool for coming in." I said shortly. God knows I had tried to persuade her otherwise.

Graves shook his head again. "No. She's dedicated. Oh, she'd laugh at you if you told her so, but she is – you can tell, she cares about politics, about O'Mahony. She hero worships Fields. It must be a big break for a young woman like that, being taken on as Fields' replacement."

He grinned again. "You can't help liking her. She gave us the lowdown on Gillespie like she was a member of the investigating force."

"Huh." I was pretty sure I could dislike her if she turned out to be withholding more information. "Well, does this change anything?"

"Only in the sense that it reconfirms a link we already knew. Here's how I see it." He settled himself in his chair and began, "Jacobs stayed back to confront Damian Fitzpatrick about something. I suspect that something has its roots in Fitzpatrick's dealings with Gillespie, over land and probably this benighted M3 road. Jacobs leaves, Fitzpatrick then has a meet with whoever it was who murdered him – and it's not too big a leap to assume that he contacted this person on the back of his confrontation with Jacobs."

I nodded. It made sense – "hung together" as Locke would say. "Okay. So, who did Damian Fitzpatrick contact between Jacobs leaving him and the estimated time of death at…" I checked the notes. "eleven forty."

"That's just it." Graves huffed. "No one. No calls in or out of his mobile, no emails, no land line calls."

"Okay. Then, the meeting was set up before the confrontation with Jacobs."

MacPherson threw us over a file marked "Patrick Gillespie."

"This is where it all comes together." She pointed at the file.

"Gillespie. He has links to every person in this, from Rory Fitzpatrick to An Taoiseach. Look. His son Dominic went to college with Rory Fitzpatrick. Rory did work experience in one of Gillespie's companies. Damian and Gillespie have been linked for years – the dogs on the street say Damian fed him information on deals and projects whenever he could. The boys in special crimes say our late Minister may even have fed him information on investigations."

"O'Mahony comes into it in a slightly different way. He and Gillespie have been at loggerheads for years – he's the one big developer in Ireland that O'Mahony won't get into bed with. Fields, we now know from Caroline, is a major force behind this policy. He hates Gillespie – which incidentally makes me like the man a whole hell of a lot more."

She tilted her chair back so far it was a wonder she didn't go right over. Bouncing on it slightly she continued, "Jacobs was involved in the motorway from the beginning and deeply bitter about the way the M3 route was gerrymandered. He hates Gillespie. He hates the corruption that seems to surround all these decisions. And he ends up working closely with the Minister who may well have aided this corrupt sewer rat in screwing over the country."

Graves took up the thread. "Jacobs puts pressure on Fitzpatrick. Fitzpatrick and Fields have an almost public row about his involvement with

Gillespie. It all looks as if it's about to become very public unless he does something about it. He moves to get himself taken off Rory's company – to protect his son we assume. Maybe we can take from that that Rory was also putting pressure on him?"

Claire frowned. "Yeah. It seems likely. But – there's something about those papers being stolen that kind of worries me. But anyway, putting that aside for the moment, the pressure mounts and Damian wants out. So – someone, who has everything to lose from Damian chickening out, moves swiftly and kills him."

"Gillespie is at the back of it. Whoever actually did it, he'll have set it up." I finished.

Graves nodded at Claire and me.

"Off you go. Go talk to Gillespie." It was the moment subconsciously we had all been waiting for. Out of the fog and mist of this bizarre case we had a suspect and one we could relish. Claire had her coat on before I could stand up.

Gillespie's house – like Elaine Dunne's – was in one of the new, exclusive suburbs that sat on the hills above the city, dragging motorways and convenience stores after them into what once were rural villages.

Unlike the Dunne's home, the property developer had not compromised his own personal taste one iota to conform with modern stylishness. His was a huge vulgar ranch of a place, with white pillars stuck incongruously onto a house that was too modern for them and statues of pseudo-Grecian beauties stuck randomly around the huge garden.

It was a glorious monument to one man's bad taste – a real criminal's dream house.

"Christ." Claire whistled through her teeth. "It's awful, isn't it?"

"It's South Fork meets Disney world." We crunched our way up to the front door over thick gravel. We were greeted by ferocious barking and a harsh male voice yelling "Who is it."

"DS Doyle, Special Branch." There was no point in pleasantries where Gillespie was concerned.

He was as thick and bullish as they came and only his wife – a shrew from

Limerick whose temper was legendary – could keep any check on him.

There was a slight hesitation on the other side of the door then it opened and Gillespie himself stood there, each hand tightly gripping the collar of a Doberman. "Put away the dogs," Claire said calmly, "Lock them out back or something."

"This is their home," Gillespie spat. "Why should I lock the poor beasts up? What do you want?"

"We want a chat, Mr. Gillespie." She smiled. "And we need to come in to have it. Lock away your dogs."

For a moment, I thought he would let them off the leash, his hands certainly twitched but there was something about MacPherson's unflappable demeanour that got through to him. Possibly he realized she'd rip his ears off if he made her hurt a dog. At any rate, we were made wait while he disappeared into the back of the house, but he finally returned without the dogs and ushered us into the drawing room.

It was the perfect interior to complement the exterior, that's all I can say about it. Chandeliers, ornaments, chintz, a mish mash of styles and colours. Hideous. And an all-pervading smell of damp dog.

"Well?" Gillespie threw himself into a chair and growled at us. He was a huge man – a muscle bound monster in his day but now running to fat.

He had a heavy featured cunning face; without doubt he was a smart man, street smart, and I had heard he could be charming to men as well as women when he wanted but that was a side he didn't bother wasting on the Gardaí.

"Mr. Gillespie." Claire MacPherson managed to put just about every ounce of contempt possible into those two words. "We want to have a little chat with you about an old friend of yours. Someone you used to have extensive dealings with, someone you were very close to."

She smiled a little shark smile and sat herself down on the edge of a plush armchair. "Damian Fitzpatrick." I watched Gillespie closely. There was no doubt the name rang some bell, but I had the oddest feeling that at the same time, something had made Gillespie relieved.

"Damian? Poor auld Damian. What about the poor fella?" Only he didn't use fella. His language was peppered with curses, both vehement and colourful.

"That's the man. You and Damian, very close over the years wouldn't you say? Friends since the eighties from what we hear. Damian went higher and higher though, Minister for Justice no less. Whereas you…"

She cast a disparaging glance around Gillespie's over-stuffed drawing room. Gillespie bristled; she'd struck a nerve.

"What the —- do you mean by that?" he growled. "Damian Fitzpatrick might have been a success in his own way but what do you mean by comparing him to me? Look around you. I'm the most successful property developer in Ireland, little girl, and don't you forget it. I buy and sell men like Damian Fitzpatrick, ay, and his stuck-up little weasel of a leader, Michael T O'Mahony." He sneered that name out with contempt. "I eat them sorts for breakfast and crap what's left out before lunch."

Claire laughed. "Wow."

She regarded him with what seemed unfeigned amusement. "Get down off the high horse Patrick. You're Ireland's most successful criminal, that I'll grant you. But developer? Success? You're one step up from those idiots shooting each other on the streets of Limerick." She shook her head and chuckled. "Damian Fitzpatrick might have had his faults, but he died a Minister of State, respected, loved by his family -"

There! An unmistakable twitch at the side of Gillespie's eye as a vein throbbed.

MacPherson continued, "…lauded by the press, whereas you're lucky not to be in Mountjoy Gaol. So, spare us the outraged citizen act and let's have a grownup conversation about this, what do you say?"

Gillespie's eyes had narrowed to slits and his face was almost purple. I moved a little closer to my colleague in case he decided to do what he so obviously wanted to do and lunge at her.

"Who do you think you are coming into my home …" Gillespie raged for a full five minutes while Claire regarded him impassively. When he finally ran out of invective she shrugged and started again.

"So, you and Damian. Must have been an awful land when he decided to pull out of your little deal eh? No more information flowing from the inside, no more tip offs. Must have made you very angry, eh Paddy?"

For a moment, I thought Gillespie was literally going to have a fit but at the last moment his eyes relaxed and he sat back.

"You're some little wagon, aren't you?" he sounded half admiring. Claire smiled her sharky little grin again.

"OK, so you want the low down on Fitzpatrick. I want to make it clear; you understand, I know nothing about it at all. Have no idea what yiz are going on about. None. But – if I were to hazard a guess, about Damian and his activities, only a guess you understand…I'd say Damian Fitzpatrick was the most hypocritical corrupt rat-licker this bloody country ever produced. Statesman! Hah! Did you hear how they talked about him at that funeral? I nearly wet myself laughing. Sitting nearly in the front row I was too – I had to laugh."

He gave a gleeful, spiteful little chuckle. "Damian would have sold every one of his friends and family for a little more money, that's the god honest truth. He lived to prosper – he really did. He had a finger in every pie, in every deal. And his family? He kept that poor eejit Liam on a string for years, treated him like dirt. He even cut his own son loose the moment the going got rough…"

I could see the man try to catch the words as they flew out of his mouth; he gave a slight cough and added "Well, so I heard anyway."

32

Chapter Thirty-Two

"That's very interesting, Patrick," Claire said companionably. "Tell me now, what exactly happened between Rory and Damian?"

For a man with a lot to say a minute previously Gillespie went noticeably quiet.

"Come on, don't be shy. Here. Let me have a stab at it." This was the moment – I watched Gillespie as closely as I could without him realizing. He was so intent on Claire, insolent and contemptuous, he barely seemed to see me in the room.

"Damian was up to his ghoulies in it with you…oh, sorry, with corrupt practices and people, naming no names. His game was to tip off - let's say a major developer," her voice dripped contempt, "One with criminal connections, about every land deal, road project, motorway extension going. All very traditional in Irish politics, I have to say. Reprehensible but hardly that unusual."

"But Damian is also ploughing his own furrow and he's climbing higher and higher. Minister for Justice…that's some position to end up in. Especially when your friends along the way haven't always been the most upright and savory."

"And Damian has a son, whose business is development. Land and property. Who did his apprenticeship, as it were, in one of your companies. Who is friends with your son. Rory Fitzpatrick was a different proposition altogether from Damian, wasn't he? I would say he didn't mind at all about the dodgy land deals. Why should he? It's part of the way you people do business. But that wasn't all, was it? Damian had gone one step further, one step closer to the edge."

Claire leaned forward and stared at Gillespie. "Damian Fitzpatrick abused his position as Minister for Justice, didn't he? He made sure that you knew about the Garda investigation. We wondered how you were always one step ahead of the game. Fitzpatrick crossed a line with you that went beyond mere corruption. He told a subject of a criminal investigation inside information he received as a privilege of his Ministry. And Rory wouldn't swallow that, would he?"

There it was again. The relaxation around the eyes, the release of tension around the mouth.

I could feel how close we were to the truth, but something was off. Gillespie was relieved again; somehow, I got the sense that he thought he had dodged a bullet. I wanted to walk outside, sit in the car and mull it over until it made sense, but we weren't finished yet. Claire gave me a glance that said she felt it too, the wrongness of the scenario we had confronted him with but like a pro she kept up the pretense of arrogance.

"And there you go, Patrick. We know the story. What it leaves us with is a dilemma though. See, once Rory confronted his father, Damian wanted out. It was getting too hot anyway. Other people were getting suspicious. So, he backed out, didn't he? And you couldn't have that."

Gillespie gave her a sharp glance. "What's that supposed to mean?"

"Oh, come on, Gillespie." I snorted and Claire laughed derisively. "You had Damian Fitzpatrick murdered. At his desk, the poor sod."

Gillespie's face was a picture. "Murdered? What the – Fitzpatrick wasn't murdered." He looked genuinely confused.

"He's very convincing, isn't he?" Claire grinned.

"Now you just look – I didn't know Damian was murdered." I doubt Gillespie had ever panicked in his life, but he looked possibly as close to it as he had ever come. He opened his mouth to speak and stopped dead. A look of mutinous anger settled over his face. "Out!" he roared. "Get the – Get out of my house."

With commendable poise Claire stood up calmly and said, "We'll be going for now, Mr. Gillespie. But we'll be back. If I were you, I would have a long hard think for myself. You're involved, you're up to your neck in this. And the storm is about to break – when the press hear that a Minister of State was murdered and that Ireland's "leading developer" is involved, hah! You'll be lucky if you get a trial."

With that she spun on her heel and marched out. It was a slightly dramatic exit, but I felt she carried it off. Gillespie looked thoroughly sick and confused and angry. At least the visit had yielded some result right there.

* * *

In the car, Claire was silent. I was too; the wheels were turning inside. Rory, Damian, Patrick – that was the unholy trinity. I knew we had it almost right, I could taste it. But there was something, we had missed something.

"Rory." Claire's voice was quiet but excited. She stirred in the passenger seat and started tapping the dashboard. "Rory. I think I see it."

I pulled over onto the hard shoulder, ignoring the outraged horns and cursing drivers behind us. I twisted in my seat and stared at her. "Go for it."

"We're right about Damian right up to the point where we accused him of feeding Garda investigation information to Gillespie. I know we are. He didn't even bother denying it. But that's where it went wrong. He looked – smug. Sly and smug. It wasn't Damian Fitzpatrick who sold information about Justice department operations. It was Rory."

"Think about it," she urged. "Rory has access to all kinds of information through his dad. They're as thick as thieves. Damian tells Rory that they have to back away from Gillespie, because the Gardaí are on to him."

It took shape in my head. "Rory doesn't want to. Why should he? Gillespie is the golden goose for him. He pumps his dad for information; Damian tells him all about it in order to convince him how serious the situation is. But Rory just turns around and passes it onto Gillespie."

Claire nodded. "The investigation stalls, Gillespie is laughing, Rory is

180

delighted. But Fields suspects the unthinkable – a Minister for Justice sold information to a crony who happens to be a criminal. He confronts Damian."

"According to Elaine Dunne, Damian is genuinely shocked." I said.

"He is. He confronts Rory and withdraws from Rory's company. Hoping of course that if it ever does blow up in his face, he can put some distance between himself and Rory. To protect Rory or himself…I don't know which. At any rate…"

"At any rate, Damian is raging. And worried. And then Mark Jacobs pops up. Presumably wielding some information that he picked up from his old friends in Environment."

Claire nodded.

"And Damian really panics. He could maybe ride out a scandal about the M3, God knows half the country already know someone benefited from that damn decision. But he can't afford any scrutiny now on his relationship with Gillespie. Because there's so much more at stake than a dodgy land deal."

Claire beat a little tattoo on the plastic dashboard. "Rory Fitzpatrick. Could it be?"

I didn't know. But he was in and out of his father's offices, worked on his campaigns, canvassed for him, so familiar around the government buildings almost no one would notice if he was there. He knew Nick Fallon, had often picked his father up after work, or joined him for pints in the politician's favourite hostelry. It was possible. Scarily possible.

"Whoever killed Mark Jacobs was utterly ruthless." Claire said. "They walked up behind him and slit his throat. Just how ruthless do we think Rory Fitzpatrick is?"

I didn't know the answer to that one.

33

Chapter Thirty-Three

Caroline Jordan

"Crikey!"

I looked around the ruins of my living room in dismay. I hadn't thought about what state the place would be in; in some naïve way I had assumed the nice police officers would put everything back where they found it.

Instead piles of papers were heaped by the balcony window and cushions were tossed off the couch and armchairs. Through a gap in the door, I could see the bedroom looking like a bombsite and the kitchen still boasted the dirty dishes from nights before.

I looked at Rory and shrugged. "Sorry. It's not exactly welcoming."

His warm brown eyes crinkled in amusement. "Hell, it's fine. My place looks worse on average, and I've never been burgled."

He threw his overcoat across the nearest surface and rolled up his sleeves. "I'll do the dishes. You do something girly with the living room. I'll meet you on the armchair in half an hour with the Chinese takeaway. How's that sound?"

"Great." I wanted nothing more than to flop on the sofa and ignore the mess, but I suppose having some help and company was the next best thing. And it took a surprisingly short amount of time to put order on the place. One of the benefits of living in tiny apartments is that you tend to keep clutter to a minimum.

Rory was still working away at the dishes when I dragged the larger file box over to the couch and started to sift through it.

"Leave it!" Rory said sternly from the kitchen sink.

"Ah, I'm just putting them in some order." All Liam's hard work, I thought. "Your poor uncle. He was really upset that someone went after this stuff."

"Poor Liam. He really had no idea that there was anything in that pile of stuff?"

"Ye gods, no. He was distraught. He's never have given them to me if he had thought there was anything in them that could cause trouble. I was so sorry for him. I keep telling him he couldn't possibly have known."

"Of course not. Poor old Liam." He came and flopped on the sofa beside me brandishing a collection of takeaway menus. "Do you actually ever cook in that kitchen or just order takeaway?"

"Takeaway. Obviously." I pointed at the Indian. "House special Byrani please."

He grinned and started reading the other choices out for himself. "What's the korma like?"

"Divine, go for the Lamb Korma and then we can share." I gave up on the paperwork and just shuffled it together until it fitted back into the box. Rory dialed the number using my mobile so they would know the address automatically, then tossed the phone onto the coffee table. I winced. That phone was my lifeline.

"Careful with the hardware, please."

He just grinned again. He really was attractive up close. And so easy to be around. I felt as if we'd hung out together for ever. I looked away before he could see me staring at him, like a lovesick pup.

"I guess we'll never know anyway. What was in the papers I mean. Why someone went after them."

"But we do!" I couldn't believe no one had told him. "Your uncle had copies of them all. Well, not of everything but he had a log of everything he put into the box, and he took copies of a lot of things."

Rory sat up. His expression was unreadable, but I assumed he was as relieved as I had been to hear it. "Not that it got them much further along," I added, apologetically. "It was just some financial papers and a note Liam got from your dad. Sorry. But at least they know what was missing."

"Really."

He sounded deflated. I tried to cheer him up. "It's all part of the investigation, you know. I mean they'll figure out sooner or later what was important about that stuff. Once they do, you'll see – they'll be a bit closer to finding out who-who killed your dad. They really will." Without thinking I reached out and stroked his arm comfortingly. "I'm so sorry, Rory, but it really will all get sorted."

He moved suddenly closer, and my heart skipped a beat, literally. He stroked my hair with one hand. It was a warm, comforting gesture.

"Caroline." His voice was husky, low pitched. "You're so lovely. Lovely Caroline. I've always liked you, you know?" Those lovely eyes were staring into mine. "I used to look at you, bustling around Dad at canvassing, or when he was preparing for a press conference. You were always so beautiful, so calm, even when things were going into meltdown."

He kissed my cheek lightly. "I've always hoped to get to know you better." His lips brushed mine. "Much, much better…."

He drew back and sighed. "It's funny how things turn out."

Confused I searched his face. Of course, he was probably in the horrors over his dad's death and maybe expecting him to be in the mood for unalloyed romantic wallowing was a bit unfair. I stroked his arm again (I am nothing if not an optimist) and said "It is. And these are not the circumstances I would have liked. But – I am glad we're getting to know each other better."

Rory looked at me and suddenly laughed. "Yes. So am I. Here – tell me all about the break in. You poor thing, you must have been scared witless."

"I was. I was absolutely frozen. You know I always thought I would react differently if someone broke in. I have a sword – no, don't laugh! I keep a samurai sword by the bed. But when I realized someone was in the room I just froze. I lay there, and just tried to look asleep."

"It was sensible. If they'd seen you were awake- "he shook his head. "Well, it doesn't bear thinking about. And you couldn't see his face?"

"No, I could barely see him. Just an outline as he went through the front door. Just a tall figure, broad, that's all."

He squeezed my hand. "Well, it's all over now, anyway. Thank God, you didn't confront them. And at least all they took was some crap Liam left here. It could have been worse."

It wasn't quite the strong shoulder I had imagined but still, it was sympathy and after the rotten week I had had it felt good. Rory continued to hold my hand as well, which was good too. "And you don't remember the exact contents of the papers they took by any chance? I mean you had them here for nearly 2 weeks. Didn't you look at them at all?"

"Um, no. Sorry Rory, but it was hardly urgent." It was ridiculous but I felt defensive. "I had so much on I had barely time to sleep. Liam's book outline was already done, and nearly ready to be shown to the agent. Papers and records and stuff, they weren't that important right now. I planned on looking at them over Christmas – I really am sorry. If I had known they were important to – to the murders or anything…but I didn't. I never even had a chance to look at poor Mark's stuff."

"Of course not. Ah, listen to me. I'm interrogating you. I'm sorry. I just – well, I just hoped I suppose." He hugged me, "And I am an insensitive clod. I forget you were so close to Mark Jacobs. Awful thing to happen to him. What stuff did you have to do?"

I grinned. At least he was trying to sound interested. "It's OK, it was just a flash drive. His short stories, creative stuff. He gave them to me ages ago and of course, I promptly forgot. Nothing important, except to his family."

"Nothing to worry you?" his anxious look touched my heart, not going to lie.

"Nothing, not a bit."

Like a storm cloud passing, Rory's face cleared from dark to sunny. He jumped up. "Dishes! And knives and forks. I'm starving. Let's have everything ready."

"Okay." Relieved to see him back in good form, I grabbed my coat and keys. "Giri will be here any minute with the delivery. He's never late for me. I'll pop down and wait for him."

"No, No." he shook his head firmly and smiled down at me. "I'm not sending my girl out in the cold. I'll wait for the delivery – just inside the outer door? Grand. You get the plates out."

I put the keys down on the counter-top and heaved a little sigh.

It felt nice to be the kind of girl who couldn't be expected to wait in the cold for her takeaway and it felt very good to hear Rory call me "my girl."

34

Chapter Thirty-Four

DS Doyle

"Paula Hughes on line two,"

The name didn't ring any bells. Locke rolled his eyes and mouthed "Jordan's sidekick," and I remembered, a pleasant woman, efficient and very calm. Always seemed to be organizing things.

"I'll take it," Anything would be a welcome distraction from staring at the wall, trying to fill in the gaps in our theories. It was hours since we visited Gillespie and the postmortem on that encounter was drawing to a close. I took the call at my desk.

There was a brief pause, long enough to wonder if she'd possibly hung up, then "DS Doyle?"

"Speaking."-

"Oh. I – okay this is going to sound over-protective and a bit neurotic, but please hear me out." Her voice was steady, but there was a note of panic lurking in there. "I've been trying to ring Caroline and I can't get through.

Oh, that woman.

"I see. Well, she is probably fine, but I'll send someone round to check." Looney wouldn't like us using resources like that, but we had a Minister and a senior civil servant dead, no harm to be careful about the political adviser.

"Yes. No, no, that's not if. Yes, I'm telling him," She hissed…I realized she was not alone.

"Sorry, that's Stephen. Look, we're trying not to panic but…Caroline gave me a flash drive yesterday, she asked me to look through it. It was given to her by Mark Jacobs, ages ago. Back at Minister Fitzpatrick's funeral. He said it was short stories, creative writing stuff, he asked to mind it for him. She forgot about it, then when he died…she thought his family might like to have it, but Mark's stuff can be quite edgy. She wanted to make sure there was nothing too shocking,"

Choking back an impatient "spit it out," I sighed. "So…?"

"So, I only had a chance to look at it. I emailed it to you just now. Detective, it's not short stories. It seems to be ledgers, and photos of letters and all sorts of things. There also a document, written by Mark. It – it says he was seeing Rory Fitzpatrick; it says he was afraid, very afraid, that Rory was involved with a gangster, and that it was Rory who sold secrets to him, and there are lists and lists of deals and all sorts."

Her calm broke. "Rory Fitzpatrick…Caroline has been dating him. He picked her up from work today."

I signaled frantically to Claire and Locke, while trying to wrestle my email open with my free hand. MacPherson pushed me aside impatiently and tapped keys furiously until a word document appeared. She was a fast reader and even quicker on the uptake. "Damn, damn, damn!" She was up and moving for the door before I'd had time to scan the first paragraph. "Jordan's address," she snapped, "And get uniforms moving too." Locke and I moved at the same time, chasing behind her.

"Dear Caroline," Locke read aloud, sitting in the back seat with my phone, as the Dublin city scape blurred past in the dark.

"It's all been such a horrible mess; I am still not even sure what I will do about it. You asked me recently if I thought I would ever meet anyone, someone permanent, and I wanted to tell you then. I wanted to explain about Rory, it broke my heart to keep our relationship secret, but he was so afraid of his parents finding out. He couldn't tell Margaret he was gay at all. Damian didn't care, in fairness to him, but he would have hated him dating me.

Caro. I found these in Rory's house. They go back years. He's in every dirty deal, up to his neck. And worse. There's much worse. He leaked the information to Gillespie that sank the Garda investigation. There's no doubt.

I've written it all out. My last report, Caro. I am going to talk to him about it as soon as I can. I am going to ask him, for my sake, to come clean. If he can do that, if he can put some of this right I'll resign, I'll wait for him, and we can have a decent, clean future. If he won't, then I'll have to decide what to do. I know what I should do. I just don't know if I can. I hope you don't have to read this but in case anything happens to me, at least you'll have it. You've always been the only one I could really trust…."

The poor, poor fool," he added quietly. "He was so mad about Rory, he thought he could get him to come clean."

35

Chapter Thirty-Five

aroline Jordan

Rory's insistence on meeting the takeaway at least gave me a chance to check my phone. The screen was blank, which almost stopped my heart. Had he actually damaged it, tossing is on the hard surface like that? Nope, thankfully, the eejit had turned it off by accident. Or design. Maybe he didn't want us to be interrupted by the inevitable phone call full of disaster laden news, the new normality of my life.

On impulse I decided to tidy the bedroom. Did I mention I am an optimist? I did a mad dash around the room, throwing bedclothes back on the bed and laundry into the wicker basket in the bathroom.

True to form my phone rang as I tried to stuff a pile of jackets and scarves back into the wardrobe.

"Stuff it." I gave up the unequal struggle and threw them into the utility room instead. Slightly out of breath I picked the phone up on its last ring.

"Hello?"

"Caroline?" it was DS Doyle. He sounded strange, the echoey sound of a phone over Bluetooth. In a car, I realized. "Caroline, where are you?"

"At home! Why? What's wrong?" the familiar horrible, panicked feeling suddenly flooded back into the pit of my stomach. What had happened now? "Is something wrong?"

I heard him take a measured breath at the other end of the line. "Caroline.

Are you alone?"

"Yes, Well, no, I mean Rory Fitzpatrick is here, but he's just stepped out."

There was a sharp intake of breath from Doyle. "Yes, Paula told me you left with him. Caroline, I want you to listen to me. If Rory is still out, lock the door and don't let him back in. Don't argue, just do it."

I opened my mouth to argue but stopped myself. Trying not to let my knees shake too much I grabbed the keys and locked the door from the inside.

"I've locked it. Now – tell me why."

"We're on our way over, Caroline. Look it's too hard to explain on the phone but we have to talk to Rory Fitzpatrick, urgently. Don't let him in. Just be patient, we're almost there. But whatever you do don't open the door until we get there."

And he hung up.

Mother of…! Maybe Giri would be delayed, and Doyle would get to the lobby of my building before Rory came back upstairs and found I had locked him out. How on earth was I going to explain that I had just locked the door against him because Doyle told me to? Come to that, why had I just taken Doyle's word for it? There was something compelling about the way he had spoken, not dramatic but quietly convincing.

But Rory! Oh, for god's sake what was I thinking? I half moved towards the door to unlock it, feeling like a perfect fool for having locked him out in the first place. Just as I did the handle turned and I heard Rory push against the door.

"Caro?" he called out.

"Rory!" I bit my lip. "Rory, is that you?"

"Caroline. It's me. Hey. Open the door."

"Um. I can't. I mean – look, I know this seems really odd, but I can't let you in…"

I put my ear to the door and listened. "Rory? Rory, can you hear me?" Silence. Confused I stepped back. "Rory?" I called out louder but there was absolutely no sound from the other side. I was tempted to open the door and be done with it.

Maybe Doyle had arrived, and Rory had just moved down the corridor to talk to him? I strained to hear any sound from outside but there was nothing.

"Rory?" I tried again.

Suddenly to my horror there was the sound of a key in the lock. My lock, on my door. Instinctively I glanced around and saw my own set of keys on the counter-top where I had left them.

I might be slow on the uptake but even my brain started sending out alarm signals at this.

Samurai sword! I made a dash for the bedroom and almost made it – the front door swinging open behind me, I heard running steps and then a stinging pain on the side of my head. I stumbled and fell, twisting as I did so. I could see Rory above me, his face distorted in anger, hands grabbing at me as I slapped them away.

"You stupid little cow" He spat. "Why the hell couldn't you have just kept out of it."

I tried to squirm away from him, but he easily restrained me. I felt another sharp blow on the side of my head as he punched me. It was the most sickening sensation I had ever experienced.

"Stay still," he panted, and his hands pressed me down against the carpet. It was pointless trying to struggle with him, he could easily knock me out with one more blow. I forced myself to go still; he hit me again but without half as much force.

"Please," I said trying not to cry, "please, Rory." He shook his head in distaste.

"Stop it. Shut up." But he loosened his grip on my hair very slightly. "I knew it. I knew you knew something. You remembered what was in those files didn't you."

I shook my head and then stopped. The alternative was telling him that Doyle was on the way. He caught my face in his hand and forced me to look at him.

"What was it?" he almost shrieked. The solid, good-natured mask had burnt away, his real face twisted and angry beneath.

"What? Was it that blasted letter? The stupid old fool, he just couldn't resist it. He had to make sure Liam knew it was me who screwed up. Did Liam tell you what was in it? Did he? How my dear old dad told him that he wanted to make sure the great Damian Fitzpatrick wasn't linked to anything shady. Shady!" he rubbed his hand across his face – his gloved hand I registered with shock. "Dear old Dad."

"He didn't" I managed. "He just said he hoped it would look as if he was a sleeping partner."

Rory slapped my face and the tears started to course down my cheeks.

"Shut. Up. Don't you think Liam would have figured it out? Or you? Once he saw how much my dad lost by pulling out, they were bound to realize. Why the hell did he have to start writing that book?"

He pointed a finger at me. "You. You put him up to it."

"You killed your dad," the words escaped involuntarily. "And Mark. Oh God. You killed poor Mark. You slit his throat."

"Stop it." He roared. "I told you to shut up."

Suddenly – and it was a truly dreadful sound- he giggled.

"I did, though. I did. I did. Oh dear. Poor Dad. Gillespie would have killed me though if it had all come out. I really didn't want to do it, but I had no choice. It was just so unfair. After everything Dad did, he suddenly gets squeamish just because I let Patrick know the cops are onto him. You should have heard him. He went on and on, like he never did anything in his life."

A shadow moved behind Rory. I caught my breath.

"I am sorry about Mark though." He said, suddenly changing mood again. "I really liked him. He was so earnest, so upright. I only meant to get close to him, keep him sweet. But I really liked him in the end. He was so mad about me, it was sweet." His grip tightened again, and a fresh wave of pain almost pulled me under, into darkness. "I had absolutely no intention of hurting him, none, but the moment O'Mahony called for an investigation I knew Jacobs would some forward, bleating about Tara and the motorway. I really am sorry about it though. I'm sorry," he stroked my cheek, "So sorry you had to see that, poor Caroline."

I shifted, trying to get some breath into my body. He was leaning on my chest, and it hurt. "Please, Rory."

He shook his head. "I'm sorry," He drew his hand back clenched into a fist.

"I need to get away Caroline, I do. I am sorry."

I screamed inside as his fist thundered towards me – flinching against the blow, I missed what happened next, I was only aware that somehow the thump never landed and the pressure of Rory's knees on my chest suddenly lifted. My eyes were stinging from tears and pain, but I could see the garda, Claire, swinging at him with her baton, hear the roars out of him as blow after blow landed.

Clutching one arm he went down. I went down too, into a soft well of unconsciousness for a merciful moment, all too brief. Somehow, I felt two pairs of hands grabbing my arms and I screamed. Or due to ongoing lack of oxygen and excruciating pain, I squeaked loudly.

"It's OK, it's OK," MacPherson's calm voice sounded in my ear. I opened my eyes in time to see a red-faced Doyle handcuffing Rory on the floor, his knee stuck in the small of Rory's back as he wrestled his arms backwards.

I hoped it hurt like hell.

36

Chapter Thirty-Six

DS Doyle sat opposite me in the offices of Jordan PR while Paula and Stephen fluttered around him like acolytes at a temple.

Ever since the night he had arrested Rory at my apartment my loyal troops had spoken about him in the awestruck tones usually reserved for demigods and Pierce Brosnan.

The only person higher in their estimation was Detective Claire MacPherson and frankly I agreed. I had developed a massive girl crush on her, something about the way she swung a baton. I was also very sure I owed her my life; Doyle having explained how she grasped the situation and was out the door before he'd fully digested what Paula was saying.

My heart was also full of gratitude to Paula and Stephen, for that call and many other reasons. The days after Rory's arrest had not been pleasant, made bearable only by real friendship.

"I can get more biscuits!" Stephen offered, eyeing the offering piled high with a dubious expression. Presumably, he worried that the selection of sixteen different brands of fabulous chocolate confectionery he had magicked from some hidey hole would not be sufficient. DS Doyle looked embarrassed as well he might. Never had a man been fawned on to such a degree.

"No, no thanks. This is fine!" He grabbed an Elite chocolate Kimberly and tried to look suitably enthused. "Um, thanks."

"Out." I ordered. "Out the pair of you." Doyle looked relieved.

"I'm sorry about that. They just want to thank you, you see. And around here Chocolate biscuits are the symbol of greatest status."

"I see." He smiled, which made him look if not warm and friendly, at least less stern and scary. While my opinion of him had risen rapidly, there was no denying he was a difficult character.

"Anyway. I just wanted to let you know what's happening. About Rory and all."

I looked at him steadily. Over the previous three months I had learned to hear that name spoken without shuddering. I was proud of my self-control. I had spent most of Christmas holed up in my mother's house while Derek Fields assured everyone, I was abroad, relaxing and recovering. Actually, it was Mother who was abroad, doing just that. A pained note left on the mantelpiece informed me I was welcome to house sit, but the notoriety I had caused was so painful, her doctors had recommended rest in a warmer climate.

"Florida, I hope," Paula had said. "Plenty of other alligators for her to hang out with!"

By unanimous agreement, Fields had stayed on past his proposed retirement date to help O'Mahony weather the worst political scandal in the history of the state. He rang me almost daily, with some gossip or to "run something past me."

At first, I just stayed where I was, hidden under a duvet, trying not to listen to the news but despite myself I got interested in the glimpses of Fields' strategy –He had O'Mahony out front and performing like a seal at a fish supper. The full gamut of human emotions, or a reasonable approximation of same; sorrow at the fall from grace of a dear colleague's memory; outrage at his now exposed corruption; horror at his son's betrayal and anger on behalf of poor Mark Jacobs.

I had a brief relapse when Mark's mother called in person, my heart broke over again, but she left me with a stern warning to get on with life. "Mark would hate to see you like this," she said bluntly. "Get up and get dressed, at least. And come visit me and his Da when you feel able." Jerry, his dad, was pretty much bed ridden now.

And the days ground by. I pretended to everyone including Paula that I was going to family on Christmas Day, instead I just ate horribly expensive takeaway from a posh restaurant and read my mother's collection of Vogues and Cosmopolitans. I put them all back in the wrong order because I'm a petty cow at heart.

I knew I was on the mend when I emailed Fields to remind him to push the new legislation on Banking through the Dail while the height of the storm raged about the Fitzpatrick case. I couldn't help who I was, I suppose.

And here I was back at work, bruises healed, broken ribs mended.

"Rory had pretty much confessed to everything. Well, almost. He won't give up Gillespie."

"But he did! He did, that night. He said to me "Gillespie got me the stuff.""

Doyle gave me a sympathetic smile. "Yeah, and in a film that would be it. Bang to rights. Brave victim testifies and all the bad guys get theirs. Sadly, in real life, lawyers get involved and Gillespie has a huge team of sharks."

He had a point, I admitted grudgingly. With Rory now denying ever having said it but confessing to everything else it was a hard sell.

"Well, let's just say it's not a done deal. But – we will get Gillespie. Rory's already admitted feeding him information on a Garda investigation. Gillespie is going down for something, that I can guarantee you."

He sat back and gave me a shrewd look. "So how are you really?"

There was something about the man that made me want to be honest with him.

"Pretty crap, on and off. But getting better. Does it make me an awful wimp that I can't just shake off that night?"

He shook his head. "No. You'd be a fool if you could. But it will get better." He said it so matter-of-factly I could almost buy it.

"I also feel like a total fool, falling for Rory's line like that."

"Ah. Well, I wouldn't. Rory Fitzpatrick is a very dangerous man. No one suspected he was anything but a nice, rugby loving Dublin four type. He's a psychopath. And he hid it extremely well." He shook his head sadly. "You know what I can't shake off? Mark Jacobs loved him; they had a relationship for over a year. He was prepared to stand by him, resign his own career, everything. And Rory is mildly regretful that he had to kill him. He's mainly sorry he had to kill someone who loved him so much. Narcissistic to the bone."

"How's his mother doing?"

"Well, it's hard for the family. I mean, Damian's reputation has been dragged through the mud and his own son is going on trial for murder. I think there's a lot of sympathy out there for them too though."

I nodded and made a mental note. Then girded my loins and woman-ed up. There was something I needed to do.

"DS Doyle. I've never really thanked you, not adequately – you saved my life that night. If you hadn't warned me…if you hadn't come when you did, you and DS MacPherson…"

He cut me short. "Don't dwell on it. And we don't need thanks. And you're welcome."

Pretty much word for word what Claire MacPherson had said to every one of my (sometimes drunken, voicemail or email) expressions of gratitude. It must be in the Garda handbook somewhere.

I laughed. "Well, if there's ever anything I can do. I do have friends in High Places you know,"

He glanced at the framed photo now adorning my desk of Michael T O'Mahony smiling into the camera as he hugged my shoulders. "Taken my first day back in the job." I remarked, "I keep it there as a reminder."

He raised an eyebrow. "I'd ask of what, but I'm afraid to."

"A reminder of – everything. The things that make this job worthwhile and the things that are never worth it." He nodded and smiled.

"I mean it. If you ever need a favour, I'm your girl. You never know the next time you need to cover up an autopsy or an exhumation or something."

He laughed outright at that. "OK. If we ever need it, I'll call in that favour. Take care of yourself. And watch your back with those politicians."

After he left, I sat and thought for a while then dialed Margaret Fitzpatrick's home phone number.

"Caroline" Her voice sounded about twenty years older than it used to and she was plainly shocked to hear mine.

"Margaret. Forgive me for ringing you at home. I'm sure I'm probably the last person you want to hear from right now."

She protested weakly but I knew I was right, and I hardly blamed her.

"Look, Margaret, I just wanted to give you a small bit of advice. Remember, no matter what Damian did wrong when it came to the big stuff, when it came to feeding Gillespie information on a police investigation, he wouldn't do that. For all his faults, he wouldn't do that. And he only kept quiet about it to save his son".

I paused. "Remember that. And whatever they ask you, whatever they say, remind them of that. When it came down to it, he wouldn't cross that line. And they killed him for it."

There was a muffled noise suspiciously like a sob chocked back. But when she spoke her voice was clear and firm.

"Thank you, Caroline. You're right."

"Take care Margaret,"

"And you Caroline. And – I'm sorry."

"Don't be. Remember what I said. Don't let them take everything away. Remind them who Damian Fitzpatrick was."

"I will. You're right too," She managed a defiant note. "When it came to it, he had his principles."

I smiled as I hung up. She believed it now, or at least she could make herself believe it and if I knew Margaret Fitzpatrick, she would make damn sure everyone else believed it too. It might not be much, but she could salvage something of his reputation for his family.

I treated myself to another of Stephen's chocolate biscuit cache. After all, I was very good at my job.

About the Author

Geraldine Moorkens Byrne

   Geraldine is a poet and writer from Dublin, Ireland. Her work has appeared in a variety of print and digital media from Anthologies to Magazines. Her short story A Stranger Among Friends was one of the 2020 Cunningham Short Story Competition winners. Recent poems have been published in Gods and Radicals Anthology, and Poems from The Lockdown. Her collection Dreams of Reality is available on Kindle and spans over 35 years of poetry. She is also the author of a children's book "Puddles!"

   This is her first full length detective Novel and was inspired by a lifetime of reading the great writers of fiction. Her nervous husband lives with her in Dublin, with their two children. She generally uses her powers for good. She has three hobbies - collecting craft materials, planning to use them and actually (occasionally) making things. Her Yarn stash is now a family heirloom.

If you've enjoyed this book, a sequel is on the way – The Body Count is due out DEC 2021 and will be available from all good sites and shops. You can sign up to her newsletter (below) for freebies, discounts, and more.

Follow her Blog www.geraldinemoorkensbyrne.com.

You can also follow her on Goodreads https://www.goodreads.com/author/show/3016469.Geraldine_Moorkens_Byrne

You can connect with me on:

 https://www.celebratingwords.com/books

 https://www.twitter.com/gercelt

 https://www.facebook.com/geraldinemoorkensbyrne

Subscribe to my newsletter:

 https://mailchi.mp/a3703e884df5/author-sign-up

Also by Geraldine Moorkens Byrne

A Caroline Jordan Mystery Book two: fun murder mystery set in Dublin Ireland, 2012

The Body Count (DEC 2021)
As the banking scandals of 2012 hit Ireland, Jordan PR are about to pitch for their biggest contract yet. The Bank of Leinster desperately need help to rehabilitate their image. Caroline Jordan is ready to step in - the only problem is the body in the meeting room!

This time Caroline is determined not to get involved. Her colleagues/best friends are getting married, political reforms loom and there's an iconic art exhibition to arrange. Not to mention that Bank contract is still up for grabs. But in Ireland all things are connected and old secrets bind strange bedfellows. As she begins to realize the web of lies and scandal stretch from the art world to the board room, DS Doyle pulls in a favour - can Caroline possibly resist investigating the rising Body Count?

See www.CelebratingWords.Com/Books